LIGHTNING STRIKE!

For five years it was thought the gunfighter known as Lightning Swift had crawled off into the desert to die after being wounded in a gun battle with Harley Mossop and his gang. How wrong everyone was. Someone shot the man who saved his life, and the gunfighter with the lightning-fast hands has returned from the grave, Colts blazing. He's mad and is not going to stop until the person responsible is planted in the ground. Then from the past looms a killer — Laredo Mossop, king of the fast-guns!

Books by Brent Towns
in the Linford Western Library:

TO THE DEATH!

3800 21 0051430 8

KDN

BRENT TOWNS

LIGHTNING STRIKE!

Complete and Unabridged

LINFORD
Leicester

First published in Great Britain in 2017 by
Robert Hale
an imprint of The Crowood Press
Wiltshire

First Linford Edition
published 2020
by arrangement with
The Crowood Press
Wiltshire

A catalogue record for this book is available
from the British Library.

ISBN 978–1–4448–4491–7

Published by
Ulverscroft Limited
Anstey, Leicestershire

Set by Words & Graphics Ltd.
Anstey, Leicestershire
Printed and bound in Great Britain by
T. J. International Ltd., Padstow, Cornwall

This book is printed on acid-free paper

Prologue

I went to nowhere, New Mexico, to kill one man. I ended up killing four.

The backwater town was Miller's Rest. My name is Billy Swift. I was a gunfighter of some repute in those days. Folks called me 'Lightning' because my draw was so fast. I didn't cotton to the name much at the time but it grew on me. So much so that eventually I had the walnut grips of my twin Peacemakers inlaid with silver lightning bolts.

I stood a shade over six feet tall back then and my brown eyes matched my hair. I used to favor black pants and a red shirt, with a low-crowned black hat that cast shade over my tanned, square-jawed face.

I was there at the invitation of a man called Tobias Bennett, who'd hired me to put Harley Mossop in the ground. Well, that was fine, but I soon found out that I'd be facing four men instead of just one.

Miller's Rest was a one-street, false-front-and-adobe town with one saloon, a general store, livery, and several other amenities, but no law office. That suited Mossop and his men just fine, for it gave them free rein to do whatever they wanted without fear of interference.

So I stood there in the street, with the burning noonday sun trying its hardest to scorch every bit of exposed skin, not thirty feet between me and them four killers.

Harley Mossop was a bear of a man with an unshaven face and a large round paunch. His sidekicks were all outlaws wanted across three states and territories. They were killers, like Mossop.

There was no doubt the man was fast with a gun and I knew the feller to his left would be too. His name was Rex Mossop, Harley's younger brother. The other two I wasn't sure about.

I'd lived for twenty-five years already but as that god-awful sun beat down I didn't feel over-confident about seeing the following day, let alone another twenty-five years.

I cursed Bennett for putting me in such a position. *One man*, he'd said in his wire. One! He also said they would pay $1,000 when the job was done.

'Good luck with gettin' paid,' I murmured in a low voice.

A rivulet of sweat ran a course down my back; I didn't know whether the cause was heat or fear. Probably not really fear as I wasn't scared. I considered myself too good for that; still, there was a healthy amount of uncertainty in the air.

Standing on the warped, rough-hewn planks that covered the boardwalk were most of the town's population. All had turned out to see if the famed Lightning Swift could save their town.

'Are you goin' to just stand there or are you goin' to make your play, leather-slapper?' the harsh voice of

Harley Mossop snarled.

We stood there eyeing each other, tension building. My arms hung loose and my fingers tickled the inlaid lightning bolts of my holstered six-guns as they sat snugly in leather.

'I think he's yeller,' Rex sneered. 'The son of a bitch ain't got the sand to stand against us.'

'*You*,' I said, smiling coldly, 'I'm goin' to kill first.'

That shook him to the core. The expression on his face changed to one of uncertainty like he wished he were somewhere else about then.

My attention turned to the remaining men.

'I ain't got nothin' against you two fellers,' I said, 'I'm here to kill Harley. His brother I'll do for free. Ride or stay? Make your choice.'

They remained unmoved. The small rivulet of sweat was now a stream which started to soak my shirt. A bead ran down my nose then dripped and fell into the dust at my feet.

I looked into the eyes of Harley Mossop and the son of a bitch smiled at me. It was cold, cruel and confident. A sense of calm descended over me as I decided not to give these bastards a chance.

My shoulders dipped and my hands came up filled with flaming Colts. My first shot, as promised, punched the ticket of Rex Mossop with a .45 slug that blew brains out the back of his head.

Gun thunder roared along the main street as the three remaining killers brought their weapons into action, doing their best to kill me. My second slug found the round paunch of Harley Mossop with a loud thwack. A red stain appeared on his light-colored shirt. The big man grunted and staggered, but refused to fall.

Another slug from my left-side Colt drove into his chest and brought him to his knees. His face contorted with pain as he fought to bring his six-gun up.

Damn it! Killing this son of a bitch

was taking too long. It was like trying to bring down a bull buffalo with a damned derringer.

Die, for Chris'sakes!

The Colt in my left fist bucked once more. The slug smashed into Harley's face and he went over backward.

By then I was in trouble. I felt a bullet bury itself in my left side with such force that it made the air whoosh from my lungs.

Staggering, I switched my aim to the remaining men.

Twice my right-side Colt roared. One of them was punched back as both slugs hammered into his chest. I knew instantly he wouldn't get back up.

One man left to kill.

Pain burned through me. I'd been hit hard and I was sure the bullet was still in me.

The remaining outlaw fired his gun and I felt the heat of the slug's passing. He'd not get another chance at killing me; the Colts in both my fists bucked in unison. With a cry of pain he threw his arms up and buckled at the knees. Bright blood appeared upon his chest not two finger-widths apart. He was dead even before he hit the ground.

The rumbling echoes of those final shots died away and were followed by a deathly silence. I slipped the Colts back into their holsters. I'd worry about reloading them later.

A wave of pain flowed through my body; I grimaced and swayed slightly. The blood flowed freely from the bullet hole in my side and it soaked my clothes.

'Wow! That certainly was somethin' to see,' the awed voice of Bennett said from beside me.

'You should have seen it from where I was standin',' I said sarcastically. 'You can see the bullets as they come at you.'

'Really?'

Damn fool!, I said to myself; then, out loud: 'Do you have a sawbones in this hole?'

Bennett looked at me quizzically; then he saw the blood.

'You're wounded!' he exclaimed.

'You don't say. The sawbones?'

'Yes. Ah . . . no. The nearest doctor is around fifty miles east of here in Clear Springs.'

'That's handy,' I muttered. 'Who digs out bullets and sets bones here, then?'

There was a sudden shout from the boardwalk and I shifted my gaze to see a drunk swaying in a non-existent breeze, holding a whiskey bottle.

'He does,' Bennett said sheepishly. Shaking my head I turned back to Bennett.

'Can you get someone to fetch my horse?'

He nodded and took a roll of money from inside his shirt. He forced it into my right hand.

'I'll see to it. You should stay and get that bullet taken out. If you leave here now and it's not seen to, it could kill you.'

One more look at the drunk on the boardwalk made up my mind. 'I'll take my chances.'

★　★　★

Twenty minutes later I was helped on to my buckskin mare. I was still bleeding, but determined I wasn't about to die while a drunk mined for lead. As I rode west out of town Bennett called out from behind me:

'You're goin' the wrong way.'

'Maybe,' I allowed. But back East lived the third Mossop brother, Laredo, and he was the fastest of them all. I was in no shape to face someone like him. No, west was the way to ride.

1

'Well, there she is, son,' Mule Smith announced in his usual jovial voice as we crested a low ridge strewn with giant saguaro cactus and yellow-flowering palo verde trees. 'Big Springs. We'll be in a comfortable bed tonight and no mistake. Maybe even no bedbugs.'

Somehow I had my doubts about that. We'd stayed in the desert town more than once on previous occasions and the beds in the Palo Verde hotel were far from bug free.

I looked over at the old prospector who rode a mule named Rosie. He was aged somewhere in his sixties and had a shock of white hair and a scraggly beard. His face was a map of lines and his voice came out in a high-pitched cackle rather than a normal tone.

When I'd first met the old coot five years before he was nothing more than a blurred figure standing over me. I had a festering bullet wound in my side with the lead still buried deep. At the time I was one hundred miles from Miller's Rest, following the shoot-out with the Mossops.

I'm pretty sure that if Mule hadn't found me I would have died out there in that god-forsaken desert. I remember his vague figure as he loomed over me. I had fallen from my horse and lay in the middle of the rutted trail. Mule was passing through on his way to Arizona to try and find the mother lode that would make all his dreams come true.

He'd put his plans on hold then and there and had gone about making plans for my future. He built a small fire beside the trail, heated up his skinning knife and opened me up, releasing all the poisons and infection that had built up in the wound. Then he drove that razor-sharp blade right in and dug the slug out. Man, the pain was so bad that I passed out.

For four days I faded in and out of

11

consciousness. On the fifth day the fever broke, making it a certainty that I would live. Since then my Colts had stayed tucked up in my saddle-bags. The only gun I used was a Winchester '76, chambered for a .45-.70 cartridge.

Now we were riding into Big Springs with canvas bags full of gold nuggets and dust. Our mine was back in the Ajo Mountains, surrounded by pipe-organ cactus, three days' ride back along the trail.

Mule slapped some of the trail dust off his gray britches with his sweat-stained hat.

'Are you comin' or not?' he asked as he eased Rosie forward.

'Yeah, I'm comin',' I said. I reined the buckskin in behind the mule.

'You don't think I'm goin' to let you loose in town on your lonesome, do you?'

He cackled. 'A young feller like you wouldn't be able to keep up, Billy.'

The tough old prospector was probably right.

* * *

Big Springs hadn't changed much since our last foray into town, maybe three months back. There were a few more bullet holes in the sign above the Desert Rose saloon but that would be about it.

As we rode along the dusty main street towards the assayer's office we passed the Springs Café and my stomach gave out a low growl. It would be nice to eat something other than the beans we'd been eating for I don't know how long. Mule saw me looking at it.

'Are you thinkin' about a home-cooked meal with all the trimmin's?'

'Has to be better than your cookin',' I said, smiling.

'Ain't nothin' wrong with my cookin',' he shot back. 'It ain't done you no harm. Kept you alive didn't it?'

'Barely.'

He scowled and went silent.

We rode further along under the watchful eye of the townsfolk until we

13

reached our destination: the assayer and claims office.

We eased our mounts up to a half-rotted hitch rail and tied them there. I unloaded the saddlebags from my horse and threw them over my shoulder, then I took the Winchester from the saddle scabbard while Mule unloaded Rosie.

After I'd beaten some of the trail dust from my clothes I stomped up the timber steps and on to the plank boardwalk. Mule had the door open by now and I followed him in. As it happened, walking through that door turned out to be a mistake. One of several I would make before the day — and night — was through.

*   *   *

'Welcome gentlemen,' greeted a man I'd never laid eyes on before. He stood behind a hardwood counter on which were a set of scales used to weigh any gold brought in. 'I see you have

14

something for me.'

My gaze ran over him with an uncertain caution that I hadn't felt in a long time. There was something about the tall lean man with gray eyes and pencil-thin mustache.

'Who are you?' Mule asked bluntly, beating me to the question.

The man smiled and straightened his suit and string tie.

'My name is Delbert Jones. I'm the assayer.'

'What happened to Higgins?' I asked, noting the bulge under his suit coat where a small hide-out pistol was located.

'Moved on to greener pastures, if you like,' Jones answered. 'I'm his replacement.'

The door to a back room opened and a trim, rat-faced man appeared. He entered the room and closed the door behind him. Then he crossed over to join Jones behind the counter. Mule looked him over.

'Who's your friend?' he asked Jones.

'What's it got to do with you?' the rat-faced man snapped. His blue-eyed gaze hardened. I changed my grip on the Winchester.

'He didn't mean nothin' by it, friend,' I assured him.

'Well, maybe he should mind his own business then,' rat-face replied. He stepped clear of the counter in an unspoken challenge.

My eyes drifted down to the holstered six-gun he wore. The leather thong at the bottom of the holster was tied about his thigh.

'Don't crowd me, friend,' I cautioned.

'I ain't your friend.'

I turned my gaze back to Jones.

'Are you goin' to haul back on his reins,' I asked, 'or shall I?'

There was a flicker in Jones's eyes before he turned to Rat Face.

'Hold hard, Flint.'

The man called Flint thought briefly, then he seemed to relax, although his eyes remained on me.

16

'Now that you boys are friends again, how about we get down to business,' Mule suggested. He dropped his canvas bags on to the scarred counter-top in front of Jones. 'My name is Mule Smith. My pard there is Billy. He's the ornery one.'

With the tension mostly dissipated, Jones smiled.

'Let's have a look-see at what you have.'

Twenty minutes later all of the gold had been weighed and calculated. It tallied to a tidy sum of $3,000.

'Whooee!' whooped Mule. He turned to look at me; his excitement was obvious. 'I told you, didn't I? I told you we hit the vein dead on.'

'You found yourself a big vein, you say?' Jones asked.

'We sure as hell did.' Mule turned back to face him. 'Billy here wouldn't believe me, but I knew I was right.'

'Are you fellers the ones with the mine over at Coyote Canyon?' Jones inquired.

I opened my mouth to speak but there was no stopping Mule, who was drunk with the gold fever.

'Coyote Canyon? Hell no! We're over in the Ajo Mountains,' he blurted out.

'*Mule!*' My snapped warning came too late.

He turned to look at me and saw my face. He realized then that he'd said too much. He shook his head sheepishly.

'If you'll get our money for us, Mr Jones, we'll be on our way,' I said.

'Sure, sure.' Jones nodded and turned around to a solid-looking safe behind him.

He took out a large bundle of paper money and counted off what we were owed. I reached out to take it but a gnarled hand reached across and cut my gesture off.

'I'll take it,' Mule said, smiling. 'Thank you, Mr Jones.'

'Before you go,' Jones said, stopping us, 'have you fellers filled out paper-work to register a claim? Can't be too careful, you know. There's been a bit of claim-jumping around here of late.'

Mule's face grew as hard as granite.

'You let 'em try to take our piece of dirt and see what happens,' he said harshly. 'We've dug more than one grave out in the desert for no-good varmints. There is room for plenty more.'

'You talk a good fight, old man,' Flint sneered.

Mule stiffened and I knew what was about to happen. I placed my hand on his shoulder.

'Come on, you old fire-breather,' I said, 'let's go find us a room and a meal.'

Mule relaxed and nodded.

'You're buyin'.'

'Fair enough.'

As we walked out of the assayer's office I was aware that two sets of eyes were burning holes into our backs.

* * *

'I got me a bullet in the chamber with that *hombre*'s name on it,' Flint growled.

19

'You'll get your chance, Flint,' Delbert Jones advised him. 'Maybe sooner than you think.'

'When?'

'Tonight. You will have your opportunity then,' Jones told him. He reached into his top pocket and took out a cheroot.

'What about the old buzzard?'

'Leave him be,' Jones cautioned. 'He needs to stay alive so he can lead us back to their diggings. The gold they brought in was worth a lot more than the three thousand dollars I paid them. Smith was right: they're on to some good color.'

Flint frowned briefly and Jones caught the look.

'What's the matter?'

'I ain't sure,' Flint said, still frowning. 'I just got me a feelin' I've seen that other feller before.'

'Where?'

'Like I said, I'm not sure,' Flint repeated. 'But after tonight it won't matter much, will it?'

2

'Them two fellers are trouble, Mule,' I warned him as our boots clunked along the boardwalk.

We'd taken the buckskin and Rosie to the livery and were making our way to the Palo Verde hotel.

'There you go again,' he reprimanded me, 'always thinkin' the worst of fellers before you even get to know 'em. Mind you, you could be right about that Flint feller.'

'I'm still alive,' I pointed out.

A sign hanging out over the board-walk read: BANK I indicated it to Mule.

'You want to stop off there and deposit some of that foldin' money you're carryin'.'

His eyes grew wide, shocked that I'd suggested it.

'What? And have some damned

outlaw pass through and clean it — and us — out. I don't think so, son. Nope, she stays right here.'

As if to emphasize the point he patted the slight bulge that showed through his shirt.

I didn't like it — far from it, but I wasn't about to stand in the center of the boardwalk arguing with him. So I let it go.

That was my second mistake.

★ ★ ★

By no means could the hotel be considered flash; however, it was comfortable and mostly clean. When we entered the lobby a well-dressed man greeted us and issued us with a key to room number 4.

'It's at the top of the stairs and along the landing to your right,' he instructed us.

I looked at the steep stairs with the hand-made balustrade and then at Mule.

'You might want to find a room downstairs,' I said him. 'They look to be a little steep for an ornery old cuss like you.'

Mule set his jaw firm and gave me an indignant look. He snatched the room key from my hand. 'Pay the man.'

Smiling, I turned to the desk clerk and gave him ten dollars. We planned on staying put a few days.

'Will that cover a bath for my smelly pard, too?'

'Damn it, Billy! I heard that.'

The clerk smiled. 'At least a couple, I'd say.'

'Don't you start, Harry or Henry or whatever your damned name is,' Mule called back as he started to mount the stairs. 'It's hard enough I get it from him day in and day out without you startin' in on me. You'd think savin' his life all those years ago would count for somethin'.'

The clerk gave me a questioning look.

'Long story,' I said. I scooped up my

23

saddle-bags and Winchester and followed Mule up the stairs.

Our room wasn't overly big but it was clean. Two single beds were positioned against the walls and there was a cupboard with a wash dish and water jug on it. The window that faced on to the main street was open, airing a slightly musty odor from the room.

I dropped my saddle-bags on to the nearest bed, walked over to the window and looked out. Below, townsfolk moved back and forth and a freight wagon drawn by a team of four mules rattled by.

'Food or beer?' Mule asked from behind me.

I looked out across the desert that was slowly turning orange with the setting sun. Again, my stomach growled.

'Food.'

★　★　★

After a fine meal of meat, potatoes, beans, and gravy, we ordered the apple pie. It was still steaming when a young lady with long black hair placed it in front of us. Lord knows where the apples came from, way out there in the desert, but it was mighty appetizing. We washed it down with hot coffee, then, after I'd paid the bill, we left.

Our next stop was the Desert Rose saloon. As we sidled up to the bar Mule called out to the bartender.

'Hey Murph, set us up a couple, will you?'

The bartender looked our way and smiled. He grabbed a partial bottle of whiskey and two shot glasses as he came along to us.

'Howdy, Mule, Billy,' he greeted us. 'I heard you fellers were back in town. You all rich yet?'

Mule opened his mouth to speak but I cut him off.

'We won't be after we buy our first drink.'

Murph smiled and shook his head as he filled our glasses.

'When are you two fellers goin' to give up diggin' dirt and find somethin' that pays?'

'Not in this lifetime,' I answered. Then I added, 'Leave the bottle.'

The glass of whiskey had just touched my lips when in the mirrored wall behind the hardwood bar I saw Flint push in through the batwings. I nudged Mule and pointed the rat-faced man out to him.

'What do you suppose he wants?' Mule asked.

'Who knows?' I said, shrugging my broad shoulders. I found out a short time later when he pushed in beside me and spilled some of my drink.

'Why don't you watch what you're doin'?' he challenged. I turned to face him.

'You were the one who bumped into me,' I said.

His eyes narrowed.

'Are you callin' me a liar?'

'Nope. Just tellin' you how it is.'

He grasped my arm as I turned away.

'Don't you damn well turn your back on me.'

Slowly I removed his hand from my arm, trying not to inflame the situation any further. By now the whole room had gone quiet.

'Flint, for some reason you seem to be set on pushin' me. I already told you earlier not to crowd me. I won't warn you again.'

A cold smile split his face as he looked me up and down.

'Shoot. You ain't even wearin' a gun.' He looked about at the crowd and pointed to a man. 'You, give this feller your six-gun. Him and me have a problem to work out.'

'Come on, Billy, let's leave,' Mule said to me.

'Shut up, old man,' Flint snarled. 'He's stayin right here.'

Something deep inside me flared, then boiled to the surface. Before I knew it I'd said to Flint: 'Are you sure you want to die tonight?'

Flint was taken aback at the words.

He wasn't expecting me to be so calm in the face of his hostility. He composed himself.

'Get a damned six-gun on and we'll see how you fare,' he snarled.

'I don't need one.'

'What?'

My right hand shot out and the back of it smacked solidly against his right cheek with a loud crack. He staggered slightly, regained his balance, then dabbed at the corner of his mouth. It came away wet with blood.

'Damn son of a bitch!' Flint raged, losing all self-control.

His right hand dropped to the butt of his six-gun and he started to pull it clear of its holster. My left hand shot out and clamped down on his wrist before he could start to raise the weapon. His head rocked back when my bunched right fist smashed into his face. I felt his nose give and saw blood spurt from it.

As Flint fell backward to the

sawdust-covered floor I relieved him of his six-gun. With a flick of my wrist he was the one staring down its barrel. I thumbed back the hammer and lined it up on his head.

'No, wait,' he said frantically, raising his hands to ward off the shot.

'Get up.'

Flint scrambled to his feet, blood running from his nose.

'Now get the hell outta here,' I ordered him.

Flint put out his hand for the gun I still held, but I tucked it into my waistband.

'I'll leave it at the jail before I ride out in a few days,' I informed him. He curled his lip.

'This ain't over,' he hissed.

He stomped angrily from the saloon and a murmur began to drift around the room.

'You should've shot him, Billy,' Mule said.

'Maybe.'

That was my third mistake.

★ ★ ★

'And that's where we found . . . '

'All right, time to go,' I announced as Mule was about to explain the details of our find to all and sundry. He whirled about.

'What?'

'I said it's time we were leavin'.'

'I ain't ready to go yet; why, we only just got here.'

It was an hour or three since Flint had left. I looked about the saloon and noted that all but two of the tables were empty, and they were occupied by working girls. One caught me staring at her and her bored expression vanished at the thought of some company.

I shook my head and gripped the now drunk Mule under his arm to drag him away from the three men he'd been talking to.

'Come on, you can come back tomorrow.'

It was always the same when we hit town. The first night there Mule would drink a troughful of whiskey to celebrate the fact.

'Heh-heh. See you fellers tomorrow and we'll do it again,' he declared loudly. 'Come on, Lightning, let's ride.'

'Why do you call him Lightning?' one of the drinkers inquired.

I froze.

'I did?' Mule asked.

'Yeah,' said another man.

'Oh, yeah. Right.'

'Well, why?'

Mule stared at him blankly for a moment.

'Because he ain't no use with a pick is why,' he said eventually. 'He's like lightning, never strikes in the same place twice.'

This drew smirks and sniggers from the men, who seemed to accept his explanation.

Once we were outside the batwings, I admonished Mule.

'You got a big mouth when you're drinkin', old man.'

He gave me a hurt look, but at that

point, I didn't much care. Lightning Swift had been dead for nigh on five years and I wanted it to stay that way. Mule knew that all it took was a slip-up like tonight and it would be over. Then there was our gold mine.

'Hell! I'm sorry, Billy,' he apologized. 'You know how I get when I been drinkin'.'

'We'll talk about it tomorrow,' I said coldly.

We walked in silence along the boardwalk. Inside, I simmered like a pot of coffee left on a stove. Caught up in my own thoughts, I was oblivious of movement across the street. It was at the mouth of a darkened alley between the barbershop and the dry-goods store. I totally missed it.

Final mistake.

A rifle barked from the darkness. There was a loud grunt from beside me as the slug meant for me hit Mule in the chest. He buckled at the knees and fell with a dull thud to the boardwalk.

'Mule!' I cried out.

The rifle cracked again and the large window in the newspaper office behind me shattered. I drew the six-gun I'd taken from Flint and opened up, sending two shots across the street to where I figured the shooter was hiding.

Another shot made me stagger. My head rang, blocking out all other sounds, I tried to raise the gun to fire again but it was a lead weight in my hand. I staggered to the left a little further and fell heavily from the boardwalk into the street. After that, everything went black.

3

When I awoke I was almost blinded by the sun streaming through a damned window. I opened my eyes but a burning pain from the bright light caused me to moan and I tried to roll away. The gentle pressure of a hand stopped me.

'It's OK,' said a soothing voice, 'just relax.'

My mouth opened to speak, but nothing except a hoarse croak emanated. I tried again with the same result.

I cracked my eyes open a fraction, trying to filter out most of the light. My vision gradually adjusted to the glare and the form of a young woman swam into view.

'So, you're awake,' she said in a soft melodic tone. 'How does your head feel?'

It took a moment, then I recognized her. She was the young lady with the long dark hair from the café where . . .

'Mule?' I rasped. The image of him lying there flooded back.

'Here, drink this,' she said, holding a glass of water to my lips.

I took a sip and tried again.

'Mule?'

My head swam as I tried to sit up, but once more the young woman restrained me.

'I told you to relax. You're lucky you're not dead too.'

'What?' I slumped back.

An alarmed expression came over her fine-featured face. She raised one hand to her mouth.

'I'm sorry, it wasn't meant to come out that way. Oh Lord, I am sorry!'

Somehow I guess I already knew Mule was dead, although it still came as somewhat of a shock. Then I remembered how angry I'd been with him right before his death, brushing aside his apology to me for his mistake.

Sadness grew inside me, only to be shoved aside by an overwhelming rage. Even though none of this was her fault, I directed my anger at the young lady. My gaze grew cold as it fixed on her.

'Get out and leave me alone.'

'But — '

'Get out!' I roared.

The shock on her face was obvious and her green eyes welled with tears. She whirled and fled from the room, slamming the door behind her.

My regret was immediate, for she wasn't the one I blamed and I wished I could take back my outburst. My head hurt and I reached up to find the source of the pain. Then I felt the bandage that was wrapped around my head.

The door to the room opened and I hoped it was the young woman coming back so I could apologize to her. Instead. it was an older lady with gray hair and a dour expression on her face. I spoke to quell her anger.

'Before you start ma'am, I'm very

sorry for upsettin' your daughter.'

'There is no excuse for bad manners, Mr . . . ?'

'Billy, ma'am.'

'There is no excuse for it at all,' she repeated. 'Casey has been sitting with you since the incident last night to make sure everything was OK. Just as the doctor instructed. This is my house and I will say who is to stay and who is to leave — and Casey isn't my daughter.'

'Sorry, ma'am.'

'And stop callin' me ma'am. My name is Irene Saunders.'

'OK.' I nodded. 'Can you tell me if they got the feller responsible?'

'No, sorry.' She shook her head.

'Does the sheriff have any idea?'

Again she shook her head. 'I'll send word to him that you're awake. He'll want to speak to you.'

'Mule had some money of ours on him?'

'I don't know.'

'Thanks, anyway.'

'Now, the doctor has said that you are to remain in bed until he comes to see you tomorrow . . . ' She stopped when she noticed me shaking my head.

'I got things to do, ma'am. If you'll step out of the room I'll put my clothes on and see to it.'

'You'll do no such thing.'

'They killed my friend.'

'And very nearly you,' she reminded me.

I moved to throw back the covers.

'Wait,' she said. 'I'll send word to the doctor. If he says you are all right, then I won't stop you. While you wait I'll fix you something to eat.'

I thought about it briefly. After all, if I was going to be stuck there I might as well have something to eat.

'OK, ma'am . . . uh . . . Irene. That would be great.'

She left me on my own in the quiet room. Right away my mind began to go over the events of the night before. My conclusion was that the most obvious person to want us dead was Flint. My next question: was it of his own volition or at someone's prompting. I thought maybe the latter because Flint had been on the prod.

Bright sunshine warmed the small room. I was still deep in thought when Casey entered with a tray of food. She smiled tentatively at me.

'Irene said you were hungry.'

'Did you fix that?' I asked her.

She nodded.

'Thank you,' I said and apologized for my earlier behavior.

She left me to eat the meal. I hadn't been at it long before the sheriff interrupted. His name was Jubal Murdoch. He was a large, middle-aged man with dark hair and a deep voice. I'd talked to him on one other occasion when Mule and I had been in town.

'How are you feelin', Billy?'

'My head hurts,' I told him truthfully.

'You're damned lucky it's still there to hurt,' Murdoch told me grimly. 'Tell me what you remember.'

When I'd finished, he asked me if I'd got a look at the shooter. I told him no. Then I asked him about the money that Mule had. His answer:

'What money?'

I gritted my teeth as my anger built once more.

'Mule was carryin' three thousand dollars.'

Murdoch's jaw dropped.

'Son of a . . . Really?'

'Really.'

'What in the hell was he doin' carryin' all that money around?'

'He was too damned ornery to put it in the bank,' I explained. 'His thinkin' was that if the bank was robbed, whoever did it wouldn't get our money if it wasn't there.'

'Who knew he had it?'

'I did, the assayer, and Flint,' I told him. 'I don't think Mule let it slip to anyone but I can't be sure. He was three sheets to the wind when I dragged him out of there.'

'Wasn't there some trouble in the

saloon last night?' Murdoch asked.

'Yeah.' I told him about Flint.

'Do you think it could have been him that bushwhacked you?'

'I don't know,' I answered truthfully.

'He's been nothin' but trouble ever since he arrived,' Murdoch told me.

'What's his story?'

'He is hired security for Delbert Jones. He arrived with Jones after Higgins left. Skunks, the pair of them.'

'I have to agree with you there,' I said.

'There have been some strange things goin' on since them two turned up here,' Murdoch told me. 'Take young Casey, for example. Her pa had a claim out by the Pinnacles.'

The Pinnacles was a group of peaks that seemed to rise out of the desert. Mule and I had first dug there when we came to Arizona, but we found very little color.

'Almost two months ago he found a good quartz vein over there and was startin' to pull out some fair-sized nuggets,' Murdoch continued. 'Anyways, it wasn't long after that when Casey went out there to see him and found him shot dead. I looked around but couldn't find much to go on. When Casey went to check up on the claim she was told that he'd never filed one.'

'Had he?' I asked.

'She said he had. Not long after that the claim was filed upon by a stranger, who then left. I took a ride out there to look about and there's no one out there. Previously another old prospector disappeared. He had a claim out by Apache Tanks. They blamed the Indians for it but there was no evidence.'

'And you think Jones and Flint are behind it?'

'Damn sure of it.'

'I guess I'll pay them a visit when I get out of here.'

'You stay away from them,' Murdoch ordered me sternly. 'I'll get to the bottom of it one way or another.'

He pointed at my half-cold meal.

'You'd best eat that before it gets

cold. I'll talk to you in a couple of days.'

After he'd left I thought about everything he'd said. I decided that when I was able to leave, the first thing I would do would be to pay a visit to a couple of polecats.

★ ★ ★

'You shot the wrong damned one,' Delbert Jones cursed at Flint. 'Then you almost killed the other one too. You were meant to keep the old man alive.'

'We'll just have to follow the other feller out to the mine then, won't we?' Flint shrugged. 'What's the problem?'

Jones's eyes flared.

'The problem is: you got careless. Now we'll have Murdoch breathing down our necks. You know how suspicious he is. It wouldn't have mattered if you could have done it clean like you were supposed to. Instead, he bested you and then you bushwhacked them on the street. No guessing who they're going to blame.'

43

'What would you have had me do?' Flint snapped.

'We could have waited,' Jones bit back. 'And another thing — where's the money?'

He held out his hand. Flint just stared at it.

'Come on, Flint, I know you have it. Smith had it on him when you killed him. I heard all about it. Now hand it over.'

Flint gave his boss a defiant look as he reluctantly reached inside his vest and retrieved the bankroll. He handed it over to Jones, who peeled off two hundred dollars.

'Here.'

Flint stuffed the rest of the money back inside his vest, disgruntled at the exchange rate.

'What do you want me to do?'

'Stay out of trouble,' Jones told him.

Flint was about to leave the office when the door opened and Murdoch entered. He looked about and nodded.

'You seem to have a rat infestation

here, Jones. You might want to look into gettin' rid of them.'

Flint ground his teeth in anger at the obvious jibe.

'What can I do for you, Jubal?' Jones asked impatiently. Murdoch nodded in Flint's direction.

'I was hopin' your man here could enlighten me about that shootin' last night and some missin' money.'

'Just what are you sayin'?' Flint's voice was full of menace.

'Let me spell it out,' Murdoch said. 'Aside from Billy and Mule, there was only two others who knew about the money. You and Jones.'

'I don't think I like where you're going with this, Murdoch,' Jones said in an icy tone.

'I ain't goin' anywhere with this — yet,' Murdoch told him. 'All I'm sayin' is how it looks is all. Besides, I'm lackin' evidence.

'However, I'll eventually find some and then I'll lock up whoever is behind it.'

'You have a big mouth, Murdoch,' Flint hissed. 'You might need to be careful or someone may close it. Permanent.'

The sheriff's eyes narrowed. His face grew hard.

'It'll take someone a whole lot better than you to do it, you rat-faced son of a bitch,' he said balefully. 'You might want to choose someone you can scare the next time you want to threaten them. Seems to me that's twice you've made that mistake. The next time might be your last — '

'If you're finished, Murdoch, we've got work to do,' Jones cut in.

'I'm done — for now,' Murdoch said, not taking his eyes off Flint. 'But I have a feelin' that I'll be back.'

After he'd left Jones focused on Flint.

'This is your damned fault. Now he's goin' to be breathin' down our necks.'

'So kill him,' Flint said, offhand.

'Thanks to you we just might have to do that,' Jones snapped, frustrated. 'But for the meantime, lie low and wait for the young feller to leave town. Then we can find out where the mine is.'

★ ★ ★

'The doctor said I was fine.'

'Are you sure you wouldn't just like to rest up for the remainder of the day?' Casey asked as I tucked my shirt into my pants.

'I been here for most of it now,' I pointed out. 'He said just to take it easy and if my headache gets worse to go and see him. Besides, I've got things to do.'

Irene stood in the corner and remained silent. She knew it would do no good to argue with me. Casey turned to her and gave her a pleading look.

'It won't do any good for me to say somethin', girl,' she told her. 'He's made up his mind.'

'Are my saddle-bags here or over at the hotel?' I asked Irene as I pulled my boots on.

47

'As far as I know all of your possessions are still at the hotel,' she replied.

I stood up, stomped my feet on the floor, then turned to face both women.

'I thank you, both of you, for takin' me in when I was hurtin'. I'm sorry if I put you out but I'm willin' to pay for anythin' you see fit to charge me for.'

They were adamant that it wouldn't be necessary, so I thanked them once more and left.

4

After leaving Irene's my first stop was a somber affair. I called at the undertaker's office to see to the arrangements for Mule's burial. It wouldn't be much. A plain pine box in a six-foot hole amongst others that he would never have known.

The price of the coffin and the headstone would all but clean me out of ready money. However Berry, the undertaker, had a word with me.

'Pay for the coffin and fix me up for the headstone the next time you're back in town. I know you're good for it.'

'Are you sure?' I asked him.

'Yeah,' he said adamantly, 'and if you ain't back anytime soon, it don't matter much. It's only a headstone.'

I thanked him and left. The funeral was planned for early the next morning. I hurried back to my hotel room, aware that wherever I went eyes of curious townsfolk followed me. I didn't think, though, that they would be ready for what was yet to come.

When I emerged from the Palo Verde hotel, I wore my twin gun-rig, complete with lightning inlaid Peacemakers. The holsters were tied down on my thighs and the hammer-thongs on both six-guns were released. I had left the Winchester in the room I'd been meant to share with Mule.

The citizens of Big Springs were about to witness the rebirth of the gunfighter previously known as Lightning Swift.

I stepped down off the boardwalk, turned and walked along the street toward the assayer's office. People stopped whatever they were doing and stared at me.

When I reached the door of my destination I didn't bother with the door handle. I just lifted my foot and kicked it in. The door frame splintered and the door crashed back. I strode

50

inside and saw that Delbert Jones and Flint were not alone. A man I picked to be in his late forties was there too. He took one look at me and started for the door.

Stepping aside, I let him go. My concern wasn't with him, after all.

'What the hell do you think you're doing?' Jones snapped, his face red with anger.

'I came to kill your friend here,' I said, nodding in Flint's direction.

Flint stepped away from the counter. He showed no sign of alarm at my statement.

'As you'll see, I'm wearin' my guns,' I told him.

The killer's eyes lowered to them and he saw the grips with the inlaid lightning bolts. His jaw dropped.

'It can't be,' he gasped. 'You're dead. Everybody knows that.'

'I would've been except for that old man you killed last night.' I said. 'Now go for your damned gun.'

'Wait!' Jones snapped loudly. 'What

am I missing here? Who are you, mister?'

'He's the gunfighter known as Lightning Swift,' Flint croaked. 'He's meant to be dead from a bullet he received in a shoot-out with Harley Mossop.'

'So why is it you wish to kill Flint?' Jones asked.

'Because he killed my friend.'

'Can you prove that?'

'Yes,' came another voice from behind me, 'can you prove that?'

I turned and saw Murdoch in the doorway.

'I had a visitor who informed me that they saw you comin' this way, packin' a brace of six-guns. They also said that you looked awfully mean. Now I understand why.'

'I'm glad to see you, Sheriff,' Jones said, almost triumphantly. 'This killer was about to commit murder.'

Murdoch ignored him. 'So you're Swift?'

'That was a long time ago,' I said. 'But yeah, I'm Swift.'

'So you ain't dead?'

'Not hardly,' I said.

'They say Laredo Mossop searched high and low for you in the beginnin'. Then they said you were dead and word was he gave up.'

'So they say.'

'You'd best leave before you do somethin' stupid,' Murdoch advised me.

'I ain't goin' until I do what I came here to do.'

If I'd been paying closer attention I might have seen the look that passed between Jones and Flint. But I didn't and the next instant they made their play.

Jones dropped a scale weight on the timber floor to distract us while Flint went for his six-gun. It almost worked. Almost.

My right six-gun leaped into my hand the moment I figured something wasn't right. It came up level as the six-gun in Flint's hand cleared leather. It might have been an age since I'd handled a Colt in this way, but I hadn't slowed much.

The kick of the Peacemaker in my fist felt like an old friend as it roared to life. I fired two shots, and both took Flint in the chest with devastating effect. He crashed back against the plank wall, rattling the window. Then he slid down until he sat on the floor, eyes open in death.

Swiveling to my left I lined the six-gun up on Jones, who stood wide-eyed with his hands in the air.

'Billy!' Murdoch barked, staying my trigger finger.

'You're a very lucky man, Jones,' I said, smiling coldly at the scared man. 'Very lucky.'

'Holster the hogleg, Billy,' Murdoch ordered.

I thought long and hard about the command before I complied.

'I should lock you up for the simple fact you came here spoilin' for a fight,' Murdoch growled.

'Before you do, you might want to

take a look at that.' I pointed at Flint's fallen six-gun lying beside the dead man. 'I took that off him in the saloon last night. I had it tucked in my belt when Mule and me were bushwhacked. Seems strange to me that he now has it back.'

Murdoch looked at it thoughtfully, then diverted his gaze to Jones.

'Well?'

Jones shrugged. 'If he had anything to do with what happened last night, then I know nothing about it.'

Murdoch looked at me.

'Wait outside, Billy. I'll be out in a minute.'

I didn't argue, just walked out the door and on to the boardwalk. People stepped wide around me, anxious looks on their faces. Then Murdoch appeared.

'Well?' I asked.

'Without evidence I got nothin',' he said.

My anger flared. 'Just give me a minute — '

'Hold up there.' He cut me short. 'I want you out of town for a while until you've cooled your heels. Go back out to your mine and work it off. I'll take care of things from here.'

Every fiber of my being wanted to go back in that office and kill Jones. Blow holes in him big enough to see daylight through. Instead, I looked Murdoch in the eye.

'I'll go tomorrow after Mule is buried,' I said.

'Fair enough,' Murdoch agreed. He reached into his coat pocket and took out some paper money. 'Here's two hundred dollars. It might help get supplies and equipment for you.'

'I don't want your money, Jubal,' I said sternly. 'I ain't no charity case.'

'Don't worry, it ain't mine. I got it off Flint. If he took your money, then this is all he had on him.'

Berry the undertaker appeared as if on cue and Murdoch indicated for him to go inside the assay office.

I took the money from Murdoch and

stuffed it in my shirt pocket.

'Thanks,' I said. 'I'll come and see you before I go.'

★ ★ ★

The following morning dawned gray and wet. The funeral was a somber affair. The small gathering consisted of the undertaker, the preacher, myself and, for some reason, Casey. And the rain. Who would have thought . . . *rain* in the desert?

The cemetery was situated on a bald knob on the outskirts of town, surrounded by giant cactus. Rain ran down the inside of my collar or dripped from my nose into the mud at my feet.

The preacher went on about ashes and dust and some other prayer things, but I was too busy thinking about Mule to be listening too close. Then he said 'Amen', turned away and started walking back to town.

Casey came across to me and held

out her hand. I took it and she looked into my eyes.

'I'm sorry about your friend,' she said.

She wore a floral dress under what I assumed was a borrowed duster coat. It kept most of her dry but, without an umbrella, her hair was wet and straggly.

'Thank you for coming,' I said. 'I'm sure he would have appreciated a pretty young lady coming to his funeral.'

Casey blushed and I immediately regretted embarrassing her.

'Can I walk you home?' I asked.

'Please do.'

We walked slowly back into town, rain still falling. A slightly uncomfortable silence between us was broken when Casey asked:

'Is what they say true? About who you are, I mean?'

'Yes.' There was no point in denying it. 'My name is Billy Swift. I'm a — was — a gunfighter.'

'Oh.'

'I'm surprised you even want to be seen with me after yesterday,' I said.

'If you mean after you killed Flint, I'm not concerned about that,' she replied; the edge to her voice surprised me a little. 'He killed my father, you know?'

'The sheriff mentioned somethin' about it. He also said he couldn't prove it.'

'They did it — and stole his claim too,' she said bluntly. 'I wish you could have shot Delbert Jones while you were at it.'

I saw her red-tinged cheeks become pale as she realized what she'd said.

'I'm sorry, I shouldn't have said that.'

'It's OK, I wish I'd have shot him too.' By saying this I only made things worse.

She stopped walking and we both stood in the street with the rain falling. I could see there was anger in her eyes.

'No. Guns are not the answer. It should be up to the law to deal with them. Not you, a killer who hires out his gun. It makes you not much better than they are.'

She stopped speaking, horrified at her own harsh words.

'I . . . I . . . ' she stammered but couldn't get out what she wanted to say.

I'll admit that for some reason her words stung, but what cut more were the tears in her eyes and the fact that she whirled away from me and fled.

Looking about, I saw Murdoch standing beneath the cover of an awning over the boardwalk. I slopped through the mud and up on to it, dripping water on to the rough boards.

'I swear I'll never figure women out,' I complained to him.

'Are you leavin' now?' he asked bluntly.

'Yeah, just as soon as I get my things together. Is there any news?'

'Nope.'

'That figures.'

'Be gone by noon, Billy,' Murdoch said. 'Don't stay a moment longer.'

'Why do I get the feelin' you're runnin' me outta town?' I looked at him with some curiosity.

'Because I am. If you stay too long there will only be more killin'.'

For the second time in a few minutes a person turned away and left me standing by myself.

I rode out of Big Springs an hour later. Instead of a packhorse it was Rosie who carried all the supplies I would need.

5

Delbert Jones watched from his window as I rode out of town. He was already plotting his next move and waited until I disappeared into the gray gloom before he came outside.

He hurried along the boardwalk until he reached the telegraph office and went inside. He found Hank Harris sitting behind his desk, reading. The balding man looked up and saw who it was.

'What can I do for you, Mr Jones?' he asked cordially.

'I need to send a wire, urgently,' Jones stated.

'Yes sir. Where to?'

'Mesa.'

'Yes sir.' He reached up, then placed a scrap of paper and pencil stub in front of Jones. 'Write down what you want to send and I'll take care of it.'

62

Jones wrote out the message and handed it back. Harris looked down and read it; he gave Jones an apprehensive look. In a threatening move the assayer opened his jacket to show Harris his pistol.

'Send it.'

Harris turned away to tap out the message on his key. He had no idea that the message he was sending was to be a declaration of war.

★   ★   ★

Roughly one hundred miles north-east of Big Springs, in a saloon appropriately named the One Shot, a solidly-built black-haired man thumbed a fresh load into his Colt while his latest victim writhed and bled out on the sawdust-covered floor.

'Did you see that sumbitch go down, Lefty,' he heard a voice to his right say. 'Huh, did you see?'

'Sure, Creed,' answered a man with a Texas drawl. 'I saw.'

'Hey, Parson, did you see?'

'Creed,' the black-haired man snapped.

'Yeah, Gray?'

'Shut the hell up!'

'Sure, Gray.'

Gray Lawson turned towards the table where his men were seated and holstered his six-gun.

'Come on, we're leavin',' he told them.

Lefty Wilson, Marsh, Creed, and the Parson rose from their seats around the battered table.

'Where are we goin', Gray?' Marsh asked their boss.

Gray Lawson was a fast-gun troubleshooter who hired out to the highest bidder. The killer with the six-foot frame didn't care what he had to do for his pay. The group came as a package, so if you hired Lawson you got them all.

'Might try the Silver Strike,' he announced. 'I don't much like the customers they get in here.'

His men cackled at his joke and followed him toward the saloon doors. Behind them, the few remaining patrons breathed a sigh of relief as they watched them go. On the floor, their latest victim had ceased moving.

Outside, a steel-colored sky hung over the town. As the group surged along the boardwalk, townsfolk parted to let them through. They were passing the telegraph office when the telegrapher opened the door.

'Mr Lawson, I have a wire for you,' he called out.

The group stopped. Lawson took the proffered piece of paper from the telegrapher. He unfolded it and read it through.

'Well, well,' Lawson sneered, 'of all the . . . '

'What's up, Gray?'

'We got a job down in Big Springs for Delbert Jones,' he told them. 'And you'll never guess who he wants us to take care of.'

'Who?' asked Lefty Wilson.

'Billy Swift.'

'Lord have mercy!' muttered the Parson.

'Ain't he meant to be dead?' Creed blurted out.

'Yeah.' Lawson thought briefly for a moment, then said, 'Go and get the horses ready.'

The men hurried off to the livery, leaving Lawson there with the telegrapher.

'I want to send a wire,' he told him.

'To whom?'

'Laredo Mossop.'

★   ★   ★

'The son of a bitch is still alive!' Laredo Mossop roared. He threw the piece of paper across the floor of his small room in the hotel.

The unfortunate hotel clerk flinched at the rage displayed by the big man. Mossop turned his cold stare on the man.

'Get the hell out!' he snarled.

66

Hurriedly, the clerk gratefully retreated through the door, to leave the livid thirty-seven-year-old gunman to mull over what was in the telegram.

Laredo ran his hand through his black hair in frustration; his brown eyes seemed to glow with his rage.

'Damn you, you bastard! You're meant to be dead!' He cursed the man who'd killed his brothers.

He had to see Kemp.

He took his double gun-rig from the post of the steel-framed bed and buckled it on. He adjusted it and checked both of his ivory-handled Colts. Then he strode purposefully out the door, leaving it wide open.

* * *

When Kemp saw the six-foot-three gunman push violently through the saloon doors he knew something was wrong. He stood up from the felt-covered table where he was playing five card stud with some of the local

67

business owners and met Laredo halfway. Standing beside the man in black, Kemp was at least a half-head shorter and a lot rounder.

'What's the problem, Laredo?' he asked.

'I gotta go, somethin's come up.'

'Go where?' Kemp was confused.

'Big Springs.'

'But your job here isn't finished yet.'

'I'll come back and finish the damned job when I'm done,' Laredo said testily.

'But I've already give you half of the money you asked for.'

Losing patience, the gunfighter dug into his shirt pocket.

'Fine, I'll give your damned money back to you.'

Kemp grabbed his arm.

'I don't want the money,' he hissed. 'I want you to finish the job. We had a contract, you big son of a bitch.'

With one swift, fluid movement, Laredo drew his right-side Colt and shot Kemp where he stood. The thunderous roar reverberated around the barroom, startling those within. As Kemp hit the plank floor Laredo looked down at him.

'Consider the contract terminated,' he growled.

6

Three days after leaving Big Springs I arrived back at the mine. On a narrow bench above a dry wash was a stained white canvas tent which we used instead of building a permanent dwelling. It could get cold of a night but it kept a body dry in the times when it rained.

All the water Mule and I required we were able to draw from a small tinaja a short distance along the wash.

The mine we worked was at the back of the bench where a steep red-faced cliff rose up to around a hundred feet. We'd been searching for some time for likely spots to find gold deposits when we came across our current location. At first we found only a couple of small nuggets in the dry wash below. We worked our way along the wash for thirty yards in each direction before coming back to the original location.

After a few days of sifting through the sand and gravel there we were only able to come up with a few more specks. The conclusion we came to was that it had washed down from the cliff above during many storms over time. So we moved our search out of the wash to the cliff wall. Another day and we found a thin sliver of quartz rock with gold embedded.

That was where we started our mine. Now, after all this time, we had found what Mule believed to be the 'Big One'.

Now he was dead.

It wasn't until after I'd unloaded Rosie and turned her and my buckskin loose that something troubling caught my eye.

A moccasin print stood out clearly in the powdery dust. I dropped my right hand to the butt of the Peacemaker and scanned the desert. While I did so my mind drifted back to the cavalry patrol Mule and I had run into on the way to Big Springs. They had been out looking for a lone renegade Chiricahua warrior named *Itza-chu*, which, in the white man's language, translated as Great Hawk.

We were told he'd murdered his way into Arizona from New Mexico, leaving a bloody trail behind him. The troopers had said he preyed mostly on those who were isolated or alone.

Apparently, although at this time I was only guessing, he'd paid the mine a visit too.

I scouted around the bench and found a few more prints. After that I checked the tent and found everything in order, which puzzled me a little because there were things there that he could have taken.

A sudden avalanche of small rocks from the mine entrance at the top of the cliff caught my attention. My right-hand Colt leaped into my hand as I looked for its source. The cliff top appeared to be clear; only after I'd studied it for several minutes did I put the six-gun back in its holster.

Realization dawned on me then: without my partner here, how isolated and alone I was going to feel in the middle of nowhere surrounded by rock and desert.

★ ★ ★

As I forked a piece of bacon into my mouth I became vaguely aware that I was no longer alone. Someone was out in the desert beyond the firelight, watching me as I ate supper. My Winchester was beside me within arm's reach and the Colts were still strapped around my waist. The moon overhead was big but the light from the fire had dulled my night vision.

The first indication was a muted *crack* of a rock striking another. I continued with my meal but my eyes scanned the darkness for any sign of my visitor.

The roar of a mountain lion some-where to the south seemed closer than it actually was, for sounds travel further on the desert night air. On edge, I waited for whoever was out there to come into the light. I leaned over, scooped up the Winchester and jacked a round into the breech.

'You know, for an Apache you ain't very good,' I called into the darkness.

'I still could have killed you many times, white-eye,' came the guttural voice from beyond the circle of light.

I saw movement as he appeared: a tall Apache with long black hair held off his face by a bandanna. His torso was naked and his sun-bronzed skin covered whipcord muscle and sinew. He wore knee-high moccasins and buckskin pants. About his waist was a cartridge belt and in his right hand he carried a Winchester.

'Do you aim to try and use that thing or what?' I asked, indicating the gun.

'If I was, you would be dead.'

I noticed him looking at the leftover food on my plate.

'Are you hungry?' I asked him.

74

He shrugged his shoulders.

'When did you last eat?'

'A day, maybe two.'

I pointed at the leftover bacon in the skillet.

'Help yourself.'

He moved hesitantly forward, not taking his eyes from me.

'What's your name?' I asked him, reasonably sure I already knew who he was.

'I am called *Itza-chu*, Great Hawk,' he answered proudly. Then he bent to pick a piece of bacon from the pan.

'I've heard of you,' I said, nodding. 'Ran into a cavalry patrol a few days back; said they were lookin' for a renegade went by that name.'

His eyes locked on me once more and he began to raise the rifle.

'Ain't no need for that,' I warned him. 'My Colt is already pointed at your belly.'

He screwed his face up in anger.

'You play trick, white-eye dog?'

'Nope.' I shook my head. 'I'm just

tryin' to figure out if you're as bad as they say. My way of thinkin' is that if you were, you would have shot me and taken my food. My name is Swift, by the way, Billy Swift.'

Itza-chu bent down for another piece of bacon and kept eating. I guess he figured the same way I did. If I wanted him dead that's what he'd be.

'You want some coffee?'

He nodded.

'Help yourself.' I tossed him my empty cup. He caught it and filled it full of the steaming liquid.

'Accordin' to the troopers I met the other day, you're some kind of desperate killer. Do you want to tell me your side?'

'Why you want to know?'

'Let's just say that a while back I'd be dead if someone hadn't give me a chance. So now I'm givin' you one.'

Itza-chu nodded. 'Two men killed my wife five moons past. The soldiers do nothing. I kill the men, and the soldiers want to hang me from rope.'

'What about the others they say you have killed?'

'I only kill those who try to kill me.' He took a sip of coffee.

'Where are you goin' from here?' I asked, curious.

He just shrugged his muscular shoulders.

'I could use some help around here,' I told him.

Itza-chu looked at me as if I was stupid.

'You not afraid I might kill you?'

'Like you said, if that's what you wanted to do I'd most likely be dead already,' I said. 'It's your choice. Keep runnin' or stay here for a while. I'll pay you and give you food.'

The Apache thought for a while, then he nodded.

'I stay.'

* * *

Early the next morning Itza-chu and I set about our first day working together in the mine. At the same time five men rode into Big Springs on tired horses. At their head was Gray Lawson on his strawberry roan. Their arrival drew plenty of attention from townsfolk, who knew at a glance that trouble had just ridden into town.

The gang pulled up outside the Desert Rose and tied their horses to the hitching rail. They stomped up the timber steps and brushed the dust off their clothes. A man went to walk past the group when a straight arm from Lawson stopped him.

'Do you know Delbert Jones?' he asked the startled man.

'Ah . . . yes, I know him.'

'Good. Go tell him Gray Lawson is at the saloon waitin' for him.'

A look from Lawson removed any suggestion of defiance from the man, who stepped around them and hurried off.

'Come on, let's wash some of this trail dust from our throats.'

Inside, the saloon was cool but it

reeked of stale tobacco and alcohol. The bar was all but empty, except for the barkeep and one other patron present, who were engaged in conversation. The five men bellied up to the bar.

'Get us a bottle,' said Lawson, setting his gaze on the 'keep. The 'keep continued talking to the other man, ignoring the gunman's order.

'Now!' Lawson barked.

The barkeep now gave Lawson a defiant look, but moved towards him, stopping halfway to reach beneath the counter to retrieve a full bottle of whiskey. He placed it on the polished countertop in front of Lawson and turned to the shelf behind him. From there he took five glasses and placed them beside the bottle. He looked Lawson in the eye.

'That'll be — '

He got no further. Lawson's right hand shot out and grabbed a fistful of his hair. In one savage movement the man's head was forced violently down on to the counter with a loud crunch.

Blood spurted as his nose broke.

He reeled away, clutching at his ruined nose, staggering as though drunk. Lawson reached across the bar, grabbed the barkeep's shirt and brought him in close.

'The next time I tell you to do somethin', bar slop, you do it,' he hissed. ''Cause if you don't, I'll kill you.'

'I see you're already getting acquainted with the locals,' Delbert Jones said from where he stood just inside the doorway.

Lawson let the barkeep go and turned to face him.

'What can I say? I like meeting people.'

He grabbed the bottle and a glass and walked across to a table, where he sat with Jones. The others made as though to join them but Lawson gave them a cold stare.

'Go away and get your own bottle,' he said brusquely.

Their answer was to go back to the

bar and intimidate the barkeep.

Lawson poured himself a drink, tossed it back then poured another. He looked across the scarred table at Jones.

'Where's Flint? Usually he ain't too far away.'

'He's dead,' Jones said in a matter-of-fact tone. 'Swift killed him.'

'Obviously Swift ain't lost any of his speed over the years,' Lawson observed. 'What is it you want us to do?'

Jones filled him in on the first part of our visit to town and told him about how Flint had messed up and killed Mule instead of me.

'They have a mine out in the Ajo Mountains. I want you to find it and kill Swift.'

'What's in it for us?' Lawson asked.

'Ten thousand dollars. How you split it is up to you.'

'OK, I'll take the job, but we take Swift alive if we can. I got other plans for him. We'll leave tomorrow mornin'. Do you know what area the mine's in?'

Jones shook his head.

'No. They didn't say. It was raining the day he left, so if you're looking to find tracks, it may be hard.'

'The Parson can track an ant across bare rock,' he said confidently. 'We'll find him.'

Lawson poured another drink.

'Where's a good place to get a bed for the night?' he asked.

'Anywhere but this town, Lawson,' Murdoch said, overhearing as he entered the saloon. 'You ain't stayin'.'

Lawson's gaze locked on to the sheriff, who crossed the room with a messenger gun cradled in his arm.

'We might as well get things straight right from the get-go, Sheriff,' Lawson told Murdoch. 'I'm here to do a job and I ain't goin' anywhere.'

'Yes you are,' Murdoch corrected, bringing his weapon into line. 'You and your scum can fork your broncs and get the hell outta my town.'

Lawson saw something in the lawman's eyes that gave him cause to rethink. He smiled.

'All right, Sheriff, we'll ride out right now. I ain't goin' to argue with that cannon you're totin'.' He stood up from the table and called across to his men: 'Come on fellers, let's do like he says.'

The five of them walked towards the batwings, where Lawson stopped for a moment.

'Just so you know, Sheriff, we'll be back.' Lawson beamed an unfriendly smile. 'One other thing. Laredo Mossop may show up while we're gone. Somehow I doubt he'll be as accommodatin' as us.'

Lawson turned, laughing as he followed his men out to the horses.

7

Cool water from the canteen tasted sweet as I drank it down. The sun's rays were unrelenting and we'd been working hard since early morning. After the previous three days of the torturous heat, Itza-chu and I had discussed taking a break during the midday hours before going back to work later in the day.

I tossed the canteen to the Apache and he drank. He put the cap back on and threw it back to me. I'll admit I had been a little skeptical about how he'd take to mining, but he proved to be a strong worker and I was glad to have him there. He would never complain or stop work for any reason.

'We'll stop soon and take that break we talked about,' I told him.

He grunted. Then something made

him pause as he looked out across the desert.

'What is it?' I asked him, concerned at his sudden interest in what appeared to me to be empty wilderness.

'Riders,' he replied.

'How many?' I walked across to a rock where my Winchester leaned against it.

'Five.'

I stared at the vastness and saw nothing.

'Hell!' I said. 'I can't see anythin' out there.'

'They rode down behind ridge,' Itza-chu told me. 'Wait.'

Patiently I waited. Suddenly they appeared. Small specks they were, barely discernible. Five of them.

'You'd best get your rifle and climb up in those rocks over there,' I told the Apache, pointing out a clump that overlooked the bench. 'Just in case there is trouble.'

Itza-chu took up his rifle and jogged over to the rocks. He climbed up amongst them and settled down to wait. I turned my attention back to the approaching riders. Whoever they were, I was almost certain that they were trouble.

★ ★ ★

When the five topped out on to the bench I knew exactly who their leader was. I was relieved to have Itza-chu positioned where he was. Gray Lawson was trouble with a big T. I'd seen him in action once, before my fracas with the Mossop brothers. He was cold and calculating and it didn't matter whether you were facing him or turned away. He'd still shoot you.

'What do you want out here, Lawson?' I snapped.

He smiled coldly at me.

'I see that it is true, Lightning. You are very much alive.'

'I plan on stayin' that way too,' I pointed out. 'Before you and your boys start anythin', you'll see my friend over there with a rifle pointed at you.'

Lawson looked over and saw Itza-chu drawing a bead on them. The look on his face soured.

'That ain't no way to treat folks who ride in peaceable like.'

'Tell me what you want, then get the hell out,' I demanded.

'Delbert Jones wants to see you.' Lawson shifted uncomfortably in the saddle.

'What about?'

'He wants to make an offer on your mine,' he lied.

'Horseshit!' I snorted derisively. 'He sent you out here to find the mine and to kill me.'

He shrugged like a school kid who's been caught out.

'Weeell.'

'You get one chance, Lawson,' I warned him. 'You all turn around and ride out. If you don't, or you do and come back, your stinkin' corpses will feed the buzzards for the next week.'

It was written all over his face that he

wanted nothing more than to pull his six-gun and shoot me down. Except he didn't want to die. His face grew hard.

'We tried to do this nice but you wouldn't listen,' he said in a harsh voice. 'That's on you. Know this, it ain't all over by a long shot.'

'Ride, Lawson,' I ordered him.

The killer snarled and swung his horse around. He gave it a savage kick and sent it cantering down off the bench and out into the desert, his men following.

While I watched, Itza-chu came down from his post and stood beside me.

'They will be back.'

I nodded.

'And when they do, we'll be ready for them.'

*   *   *

It was Itza-chu who suggested the tactics we should adopt when Lawson and his crew showed up again. The logic of it was sound, but I still wasn't convinced that Itza-chu should be taking such a risk.

'Are you sure you want to do what you're suggesting?' I questioned him for a second time.

'Do not worry. They will not know I'm there.'

I watched him as he disappeared into the darkness — 'melted' would be a more appropriate description. One moment he was there and the next he'd vanished. So I waited for most of the night, listening to all of the sounds. The coyotes, a mountain lion, even a rattler passed by. Then, about an hour before sunup, I heard a shout from the dry wash, a scream, and then gunfire erupted.

Flashes illuminated the early morning darkness, followed by the flat report of a rifle. This was followed immediately by the sharper cracks of six-gun rounds. Calls of alarm filled the air as a small war broke out in the small patch of desert below the bench.

Drawing both of my Colts I hurried forward and joined the chaos.

It was a crazy thing to do. It was dark and I was moving towards the sound of the guns and their flashes. A shot crashed through a palo verde tree on the edge of the wash and I ducked instinctively. Another cracked as it passed close so I took a knee to gather my bearings.

There sounded a shout to my front. Suddenly a figure loomed in front of me. The faint glow of the moon gave enough illumination for me to tell by his outline that the person wasn't the Apache.

Both of my Colts roared; orange flame spouted from their barrels. The approaching man was smashed back as both slugs hit him full in the chest. Somewhere behind him, a gun thundered and bullets came my way; the snap they made as they passed me signaled how close they were.

Lunging forward, trying to find cover in the empty wash, I fell face down.

More shots flew close overhead and I decided I wasn't going to wait for a lucky one to kill me. I lurched to my feet, ran to the opposite embankment and scrambled up. I found a large rock five yards from the lip and took cover behind it.

As I lay there gathering myself for my next venture from cover, I heard a voice call out:

'Make for the horses. It's no use.'

'Gray, I'm hurt,' another voice called. 'I can't get back. I need your help!'

There was no answer. The desert became silent once more. I came out from behind the rock and moved quietly across the soft earth, pausing frequently to listen. After some moments I heard the drumming of retreating hoofs as the remaining killers took flight.

'They are gone.'

I started and swung both Colts in the direction of the voice. Out of the darkness Itza-chu appeared. I lowered the hammers on both guns and holstered the weapons.

'How many got away?' I asked him.

'Two.'

'What about the wounded man?'

'Him not wounded any more.'

'We'll wait until the sun comes up, then we'll check them out,' I told him. 'Hopefully Lawson will be among them.'

Somehow, though, I knew that he wasn't.

* * *

I didn't know it at the time but the names of the three dead men were Lefty Wilson, Marsh, and Creed. Marsh had been the one who'd taken the brunt of my Colts as he came towards me. In the light of the new morning, I could see where the shots had hit him in his chest as he lay there in the sand, sightless eyes staring at the sky.

The next corpse was that of Creed, who was the one who'd been wounded in the fight. He had a bullet wound to his leg and another to his upper torso. Both shots had come from behind in what seemed to be a case of friendly fire. The gunshots had not killed him. The slash across his throat had seen to that.

Lefty Wilson had obviously been the first to die. He lay near a boulder set in the middle of a patch of cactus. As would a mountain lion stalking prey, Itza-chu had come up behind him and used his knife. A muscular reflex action had caused Wilson to squeeze the trigger of his six-gun and that had started the intense exchange of gunfire.

'It looks like Lawson got away,' I said, kicking at the dirt. 'I was hopin' he'd be one of them. Let's see if we can find their horses.'

Several minutes later we found them tied to a small palo verde tree about one hundred yards away in a gully. We led them back and slung the stiffened bodies across them.

'What you do with them?' Itza-chu asked.

'I'm taking them back to Big Springs for the sheriff there. And — just maybe — I'll kill the man responsible.'

'Do you want me to come?'

'No,' I said, 'it would be better if you stayed here. Just in case there are troopers about.'

'How long you gone?' he asked, accepting my reasoning.

'No more than ten days.'

'And if don't come back?'

'Then I ain't comin' back.'

8

Gray Lawson and the Parson reached Big Springs the day before I rode into town. Like their horses, the men were worn out and dust-caked from hard riding. They stopped the horses outside the assayer's office and climbed down.

Lawson took his sweat-stained hat from his head and used it to slap the dust from his clothes. He placed it back on his head and stomped up the steps to the boardwalk. Standing in his way was a townsman, deep in discussion with another man. Both saw the expression on Lawson's face but failed to move quickly enough; the angry killer barged between them.

One of the two made to protest but stopped when the Parson said:

'If you don't wish to meet the Almighty, I'd shut the hell up.'

The man stared at him.

'What?'

'Zebulon, chapter two, verse five.'

'Who's Zebulon?'

'I am,' the Parson said and kept walking.

Delbert Jones was seated inside, working at his desk, when the door crashed open and a wild-eyed Lawson strode in. Jones took one look at him.

'I take it things didn't go so well.'

'The son of a bitch wasn't alone like you said he would be, Jones,' Lawson snarled. 'The bastard had a damned Indian with him.'

'I can assure you I knew nothing about an Indian,' Jones told him.

'Well, he had one, and when we rode up he was hid out in some rocks. Got the drop on us and we had to ride out.'

'I see,' Jones said grimly.

'We waited until the early hours of the morning and went back,' Lawson continued. 'And they were waitin' for us. I lost three men. *Three!*'

'What do you propose to do now?'

'Hire me some more men, get back out there and kill the blasted polecat.'

'What blasted polecat might that be?' asked another voice.

Lawson turned and saw Murdoch standing in the doorway.

'I see you're still around, Sheriff,' Lawson observed. 'Which would mean that Laredo Mossop ain't showed up yet.'

'I told you and your scum to get the hell out of town. Yet here you are.'

Lawson simmered inside, but for the moment remained silent.

'You got two minutes to get back on your horses and get gone,' Murdoch ordered.

However, Lawson wasn't in a leaving mood. He stood there with a belligerent expression on his face.

'Don't crowd me, Sheriff,' he said.

'If you ain't gone by the time I said, you'll see what crowdin' is,' Murdoch snapped.

'You just ain't goin' to let it go, are you?'

'Not by a long shot.'

Lawson gave a resigned sigh and drew his six-gun. As it came up level, he thumbed back its hammer and squeezed the trigger. It bucked and roared, spitting lead at Murdoch who was desperately clawing at his own gun when the slug smashed into his chest, driving him back through the open door.

The hammer on Lawson's six-gun ratcheted back as he followed him. On the other side of the doorway Murdoch lay writhing on the boardwalk, his face a mask of pain. A red stain showed on his shirtfront, it was growing rapidly. Years of being a sheriff had all ended like this. Being shot down by a callous killer.

Lawson sighted on Murdoch's head and let go one more shot. The slug punched into the sheriff's skull and made his head smack against the planks beneath it. His eyes were wide and his body finally stopped moving.

Lawson stared down at the sheriff's

corpse, ejected the spent cartridge and replaced it with a fresh round. Then he holstered the gun, looked up and saw all of the people who'd witnessed the cold-blooded killing staring back at him.

'Looks like you'll all be needin' a new sheriff,' he said coldly. 'Yours just kinda up and died.'

Footsteps sounded on the boardwalk next to Lawson.

'Why don't you take the job yourself?' Jones asked. The killer glanced at him.

'I got a job to finish, remember?'

'Yes, but what better way to do it than with the law to back you?'

Unwilling to dismiss it out of hand, Lawson gave it some consideration; then, to his surprise, he said:

'I'll do it.'

★   ★   ★

When I entered the town the following afternoon I was trailing three horses with their foul-smelling loads draped over them. I could sense a distinct pall of anxiety hanging over Big Springs, but it wasn't until I pulled up outside the sheriff's office that I found out why.

I'd just looped the buckskin's reins around the hitch rail when Lawson appeared from inside the jail holding a messenger gun. It was cocked and pointed straight at me. Instinctively, my hands dropped to the Peacemakers at my waist.

'Don't!' he snapped. 'Your hide will be full of buckshot before you even get them halfway out.'

Cursing under my breath, I lifted my hands away from my six-guns and brought them up to shoulder level. There was movement behind him and the last remaining man of his gang came out. I noticed something then. It was so obvious that I'd been blind to it. They were wearing badges.

Murdoch wouldn't have given them badges. Not of his own free will, which meant that something had happened to him.

'What happened to Murdoch?' I asked Lawson.

Lawson's smile sent a shiver down my spine.

'He got fired.'

'You mean you killed him?'

'Somethin' like that,' he allowed. 'Now, how about you unbuckle that gunbelt of yours?'

I moved my left hand down to comply with his order.

'Whoa there, Lightning,' he cautioned me. 'Don't go makin' no sudden moves or I'm liable to become nervous and let you have both barrels.'

With slow, deliberate movements, I unbuckled my guns and let them drop to the ground.

'Step away from them,' he ordered. 'Parson, pick them up and take them inside.'

Delbert Jones appeared beside Lawson, smiling, almost gloating.

'It looks like you've got your man,

101

Sheriff,' he chortled. 'I guess you'd best lock him up ready for the trial.'

'What trial?' I narrowed my eyes.

'You killed three deputies,' Jones informed me gleefully. 'You are destined to hang, Swift.'

'The hell I did!' I snarled. 'All I did was kill stinkin' bushwhackers.'

'Easy, Lightning,' Lawson said in a menacing tone. 'That's my men you're talkin' about. However, there is somethin' you're goin' to do before you get locked away.'

'What's that?'

Lawson nodded towards the bodies.

'I figure there is enough time left in the day for you to bury my friends whom you so kindly brought in.'

I stood firm.

'Nope.'

Not one of my smartest responses, for it made Lawson step down from the boardwalk and stop in front of me. Next, he brought the butt of the messenger gun around and drove it viciously into my midriff. I doubled over, retching and gasping for air.

'I must be gettin' deaf,' he surmised. 'I don't think I heard you right. What was it you were sayin'?'

'Where's the shovel?' I said, in between gasps.

'That's what I thought you said.'

★   ★   ★

It was hard going in the hard-packed dry soil of the Big Springs cemetery, but I managed to bury the three dead men. Once finished, I was escorted back to the jailhouse where I was locked away in a cell with floor to ceiling iron bars across its front. I was dirty and sweaty and more than a little uncomfortable. When the door clanged shut I turned and looked at Lawson.

'How about some water so I can clean up?'

'How about you shut your yap.'

'What happens now, then?' I asked. 'Do I get a trial or are you just goin' to string me up?'

'Oh, we'll string you up all right,' he answered. 'The livery has a nice little beam outside its hayloft that we can use.'

'When are you goin' to do that?' I inquired.

'I would like to do it tomorrow but we're waitin' for a feller to show so that he can see it done,' Lawson explained. I was curious.

'Who?'

'Laredo Mossop.'

That was a name I'd not heard or thought about in a long time and it surprised me. It must have shown because Lawson's smile grew wider.

'He ain't never forgive you for what you did to his brothers, you know?' he informed me. 'He looked for you for nigh on two years before he accepted the stories that you were dead. I guess he sure was shocked some after gettin' my wire sayin' you was alive. Word came down the wire a while back that he shot his employer just so he could get outta the contract he was doin'. Yes, sir he sure does want your hide real bad.'

The cells and the office were all in the same room so I was more or less present when Jones entered.

'How's our little bird doing in his cage?' he asked.

'He's lookin' a mite pasty after I informed him that Mossop was comin' for his hangin',' Lawson said.

I sat down on the bunk and listened intently to their conversation. I thought that I might be able to glean some useful piece of information that could be helpful in my current predicament.

'I've been to see the judge,' Jones said. 'The trial will be held tomorrow.'

'What?' Lawson snapped. 'What trial?'

'Don't worry, it's only a formality, to look good, like,' Jones said, to ease his concern. 'The judge owes me a healthy sum of money. He can't play cards one lick so I called in the IOU.'

'All this for a mine?' I said. 'It must

be worth a lot more than we had it figured at.'

Jones shrugged. 'That remains to be seen. The gold I paid you and the old man for last week was worth more than what you got for it.' He sounded pleased with his deception. 'I'm hoping I can get at least a hundred thousand dollars in gold from it.'

'You seem to be forgettin' somethin',' I reminded him.

'The Indian?' he asked, raising an eyebrow. 'I've just come from the saloon where I met a man named Washington Murphy. He rode into town this afternoon. Apparently, he's looking for a renegade Apache who was known to be coming this way. Naturally, I put two and two together and came up with your friend.'

I'd heard of Murphy. He was a big Negro who stood more than six feet tall, with scars over his body attesting to a hard life. He was also a bounty hunter with a special kind of hate for Indians. Apaches mostly.

It was said that when he was a boy he'd been taken by a war party. How or why I didn't know, but apparently they'd treated him poorly. He'd been beaten daily, forced to eat with the camp dogs, where he'd fought them for food scraps, and had to endure other hardships. Eventually he'd been found and rescued by the army, but by then it was too late. The damage had been done.

'As soon as I mentioned your friend out at the mine he couldn't wait to throw his saddle back on his horse and ride out,' Jones continued. 'It would seem that he killed the wrong person at some time, and someone put up a two thousand dollar bounty on his scalp.'

My fingers dug deep into the cot's lumpy mattress as anger surged through me. Here I was stuck behind bars while a killer rode out to the mine after Itza-chu. I could only hope that the Apache would become aware of his presence when the time came, for right now I was no use to him at all.

9

An hour or so after dark there came a knock on the jail door and Casey entered with a tray of food.

'What are you doin' here, girl?' Lawson asked, in a bullish tone.

'I've brought some food for your prisoner,' Casey explained.

'He don't need any food,' the killer snapped.

My stomach growled at the thought of it.

'Sheriff Murdoch always had me bring food to the prisoners,' she told him, poking her chin out in defiance.

'Well, I said no.'

'Are you going to shoot me for taking it to him?' Casey argued further. 'Do you shoot women too?'

'If you keep this up I might have to,' Lawson grouched. 'Ah, what the hell! Take him his damned food.'

Casey had only gone two further paces when Lawson barked:

'Stop. Gimme a look at that thing first.'

I saw the nervous look in her eyes when she halted. Lawson walked across to her and lifted the small towel that was draped over the food. He studied it carefully before he stuck his finger into something on the plate.

'Mmm, that's good,' he voiced his approval. 'I always was partial to gravy.'

'So am I,' I snapped. 'I like it even better when you haven't put your damn finger in it.'

Lawson ignored my protest and waved Casey on. She stopped at the cell door and looked about her.

'Can someone open the door, please?'

Lawson looked over and nodded to the Parson, who moved to a hook, took down the cell keys and walked over to where Casey waited. With a rattle of metal the key was inserted and turned. The door swung open and allowed

Casey to enter with her aromatic load.

'You can shut the door if you like,' she said, looking back at the Parson. 'I'll wait until he's finished.'

The Parson looked concerned.

'Aren't you scared of him? Him being the killer that he is?'

'I'm more scared of you two,' she declared.

The Parson shrugged his shoulders and shot a glance at Lawson, who nodded his approval. The door shut with a clang and I took the tray from Casey.

'Thank you for bringing me the food,' I said.

She watched me in silence as I ate. When I had finished I thanked her again.

'I will be back in the morning with some breakfast for you,' she replied.

'Don't you worry yourself about that, missy,' Lawson said. 'He ain't goin' to need it.'

'I shall do it anyway,' she told him.

After Casey left I lay back on the cot

and stared at the ceiling, trying to figure out how the hell I was going to get out of this.

* * *

The hinges on the cell door protested loudly as Lawson swung it open around mid-morning the following day. As promised, Casey had come back with my breakfast and it had been a hearty meal. Now it was time for court.

'Out,' Lawson snapped. 'Parson, keep a close eye on him while I put these leg irons on him.'

The irons jingled softly as he held them up for display. I stepped out into the office and he put them on. He followed that up with handcuffs, then stood back.

'That'll hold you,' he said. Then he gave me a solid shove from behind. 'Get movin'.'

I staggered the first few steps before I regained my balance and headed towards the door.

Outside, I could see that it had rained during the night. The sky was still leaden and there were small puddles on the street. By mid-afternoon they would be dried up. I jingled my way along the boardwalk until we came to the saloon where Lawson ordered me to stop.

'In there,' he said, so I turned to my left and pushed in through the batwings.

The saloon was all but empty save for the judge and six men whom they apparently proposed to use as a jury.

'The jury ain't got enough men on it,' I pointed out.

'Shut up and sit down,' Lawson snapped. He pushed me toward a chair that had been placed in the middle of the empty floor.

After I sat I glanced at the judge, a short man with gray hair and spectacles. I could see his uncertainty of what was about to happen etched on his face. He looked about the room.

112

'Is everybody ready?'

There was murmurs of yes, then he looked at Lawson.

'Prosecution ready?'

'Just get on with it,' came the curt reply.

'Defense?' the judge said, looking over my right shoulder.

'Yes, Judge.'

I turned my head to see Delbert Jones smiling back at me. He was my defense. Already I could feel the constricting band of the noose tightening around my neck.

'OK, Sheriff Lawson, you may proceed,' the judge said.

'Well, Judge,' Lawson said as he walked to the center of the room, 'there ain't much to say. Swift here killed three men in cold blood when they happened by his place out there in the desert.'

'That's not true,' I called out.

The judge banged his gavel on the table he was seated at and called for order. He looked at me sternly.

'Did you kill those men or not?' he asked sternly.

'I killed one of them,' I admitted. 'But — '

'Carry on, Sheriff Lawson,' he said, abruptly cutting my explanation off.

Lawson nodded.

'Judge, I have nothing more to say. You heard it yourself. He just admitted to killing at least one of the three men. That should be enough to find him guilty.'

The judge shifted his gaze.

'Mr Jones, do you have anything to say?'

'No. What can I say? My client just admitted his guilt.'

Looking at Jones I could see the smug expression on his face as his plan came together. I looked back at the judge. Seething inside, I leaped to my feet.

'This trial is the biggest pile of horseshit I have ever witnessed. I — '

The cold steel of a gun-muzzle came to rest against the side of my face.

'Sit down, Swift,' Lawson ordered through gritted teeth. 'Or you'll die right here.'

I hesitated; my rage was threatening to make me do something foolish. Then I checked myself and sat back down in the chair. The judge turned to the jury.

'Gentlemen of the jury, how do you find the defendant?'

The jury foreman stood up.

'Guilty.'

Both Jones and Lawson smiled openly at the pronouncement. What would I have given for a gun at that point! Instead, all I had were manacles and cuffs. My eyes settled on the judge as I waited for what was to come. He hesitated, looked over at Jones, then back at me. He cleared his throat.

'Mr Swift, you have been found guilty of the crime of murder. Punishment shall be fitting of the crime.'

He paused once more and cleared his throat again.

'There . . . therefore you shall be hanged by the neck until you are dead.

Sentence to be carried out at the sheriff's convenience.'

'Don't worry about hangin' him, Judge,' snarled a voice from the saloon entrance. 'I'm goin' to shoot the son of a bitch, right now.'

Laredo Mossop had arrived!

I turned my head and saw the dust-coated figure standing just inside the batwings.

'Who are you?' snapped the judge.

'I'm Laredo Mossop.'

The judge paled and opened his mouth to say some more but nothing came out.

'He needs to hang, Laredo,' Lawson told him. 'We can keep it all legal that way.'

'I don't do legal,' Laredo grouched. Then he saw the badge on Lawson's chest. He laughed out loud. 'You're on the wrong side of that badge, Lawson.'

'Yeah, it feels a little uncomfortable too but, as I was sayin', we need to keep it legal.' Lawson smiled wryly. 'Well, as legal as possible. There are things goin' on here that Mr Jones over there would like to keep out of sight of pryin' eyes, if you know what I mean. We can't do that if you just go and shoot him down in a courtroom. Hell! If you want you can put the noose around his neck and slap the horse on the rump. OK?'

Mossop stared at me, his face dark with anger. I half-expected him to pull his gun then and shoot me, but he refrained. Instead he nodded.

'OK,' he said. 'But I get to do it.'

'Agreed. We can go do it now if you've a mind to?'

A knot formed in the pit of my stomach and my guts tensed like coiled springs inside me as I prepared to fight to the death. There was no way they were going to do it easy. Laredo shook his head.

'No, let him sweat a day or two. I want him to think about what's comin' to him.'

'Fine,' Jones agreed. 'The day after tomorrow.'

And so the date of my demise had been decided.

Of course they should have hanged me there and then. If they had, what happened next would never have taken place.

* * *

'I'm sure as hell goin' to enjoy hangin' you, Swift,' Laredo snarled at me through the bars of the cell.

'Why don't you let me out of here, Laredo?' I said. 'Let me strap on my guns and we'll see if you're as good as they say. Unless you're yellow. Is that it? Are you yellow?'

A cold smile split his face.

'I see what you're doin'. Tryin' to bait me. It ain't goin' to work.'

'Thought so,' I said flippantly. 'Just like your brothers. Only brave when the odds are on your side. I'd be more than happy to put a bullet in your foul guts like I did to your no-good kin. They were yellow too.'

118

Laredo let out a wild snarl and clawed at his six-gun. In the heat of his rage he fumbled it.

'Laredo!' Lawson snapped, stopping his draw. 'He's gettin' to you.'

'I'll damn well blow his stinkin' guts out through his backbone is what I'm goin' to do,' Laredo barked, red-faced.

'Get me my guns, Laredo, and we'll have at it,' I urged him. 'They all reckon you're some kind of gun king.'

'Shut up!' Lawson snapped.

I was about to say more when the door to the jail opened and Delbert Jones walked in.

'What on earth is goin' on?' he shouted. 'I can damn well hear you all halfway along the boardwalk.'

Laredo Mossop gave Jones a menacing look. I half-expected him to shoot the assayer then and there. Instead, he stormed out of the jail, slamming the door behind him.

Jones gave me a frosty look. I shrugged my shoulders. Then my expression changed to one of steely unforgiving.

'I'm goin' to kill you last, Jones,' I told him in a low voice. 'You made a mistake not hangin' me today. I'll kill every last one of you.'

All I had to do was get out of the damned cell.

10

The Parson let Casey into my cell that evening; she was carrying a tray loaded with meat, potatoes, onions, and gravy. A side dish contained apple pie and something else I'd never seen before but it sure tasted good.

Tonight, however, I sensed a change in her demeanor. It might have been the way she talked but her eyes kept wandering towards the Parson, so I knew that something wasn't right.

Not until my guardian had his back turned did I find out what it was.

Without any thought of modesty she hiked the hem of her blue skirt up, exposing a pale thigh. She had tied a strip of cloth around that fine thigh and had tucked a Colt into it. I swear my eyes bulged at first when I saw her skirt ride up, but then the sight of six-gun drew my attention, even though I wanted to gaze at that exposed limb.

Casey plucked the weapon from its hiding-place and was handing it to me when a voice said: 'Hey, what are you doin'?'

The Parson couldn't see the Colt from where he stood as Casey was between him and me. Her eyes widened a little and I expected her to panic; instead, she took me by surprise. She leaned in close and grasped my shirt with her right hand. She pulled me in close and kissed me.

Hard!

'Get away from him,' the Parson ordered. 'You can't be doin' that.'

Casey's left hand poked the six-gun into my right as we continued our embrace. I stuffed it inside my shirt. Once it was hidden I broke away. I stared into her eyes and saw something akin to what I felt also. Right at this moment was not a convenient time to speak of it.

The cell door swung open and the Parson came through it, a cocked six-gun in his fist. He grasped Casey roughly by the shoulder and whirled her about.

'What the hell did you give him?' he snarled.

My hand dived inside my shirt and came out with the Colt, its hammer eared all the way back. The Parson's jaw dropped as he realized his life was about to end. The gun thundered in the close confines of the jail and the .45 caliber slug took him in the chest.

He slumped to the floor, dropping his own six-gun as he went. I grasped Casey by the arm.

'Come on,' I said, 'we need to go.'

She remained frozen to the spot, her face pale with shock. I grabbed her more firmly and shook her. Her eyes focused on mine.

'Move, Casey. Now!'

She nodded dumbly and followed me through the open cell door.

I made a hurried search and found my Peacemakers and Winchester. I strapped the six-guns on, took hold of

Casey's hand and half dragged her as we went out of the building into the night.

I could hear voices starting to call out. I let Casey's hand go and jacked a round into the Winchester.

'Follow close,' I told her. 'We need to find a couple of horses.'

She clutched my arm and held me fast.

'Horses?' she blurted out.

'Yes, we need some to get out of town,' I said impatiently.

'No. I have your horse waiting behind the diner.'

More shouts followed, then came the sharp report of a six-gun. Splinters flew from the wall behind me and I raised the rifle to my shoulder. Its flat *crack* echoed along the darkened street. I didn't wait to see what happened next; I turned and followed Casey.

More shots rang out and chased us along the boardwalk. I felt a hammer blow to my side as a round found its mark and buried itself in my flesh. I grunted and staggered against the wall of a shop.

'Are you OK?' Casey cried. I gritted my teeth.

'I'm fine, keep goin'.'

I heard a voice back along the street and recognized it as Laredo Mossop's.

'I told you I shoulda killed that son of a bitch,' I heard him shout.

I could feel the blood running down my side and into my pants. From there it traveled down into my boot.

I took a step forward to follow Casey and pain ripped through my body. I gasped audibly, then I pulled myself together against the pain and kept going. We ducked into an alley but I crashed into the right-side wall of the two buildings.

'Are you OK?' Casey asked me again. I righted myself.

'I got clipped by a bullet,' I told her. It had been a little more than a clip but I didn't want to worry her. Once were out of town aways I would check on it.

'You got *what?*' she blurted out.

She stopped dead in front of me; I had to lurch sideways to avoid running her down. This caused another wave of pain to wash over me.

'Keep moving,' I hissed through clenched teeth.

Once out of the alley we came to where Casey had hidden the buckskin.

'You get up first,' I told her, 'and I'll climb up behind you.'

'But — ' she started to protest.

'You can't stay. Not now. That food tray is still in the cell, remember.'

The wound in my side screamed as I climbed up behind Casey. The pain was so overwhelming that I nearly blacked out.

'You take him,' I said in her ear, my voice coming out as a hoarse whisper.

I remember Casey turning my horse around and leaning into her back as I wrapped my arms around her waist, but not much after that, as I passed out.

It was another two days before I woke up.

126

★   ★   ★

Late the following afternoon Laredo Mossop stomped into the jail dragging a protesting livery owner with him. He threw the man to the floor and stood over him menacingly.

'Now, you sniveling son of a bitch, tell the sheriff what you told me.'

The cowering man glanced up at Lawson and returned his gaze to the floor. Mossop smacked him on the back of his balding head with an open hand.

'Speak!'

'The girl came and got his horse last night,' the man blurted out.

It took Lawson a moment to work out who he was talking about. Then he remembered the food tray.

'You mean the one who brings the food to the jail?'

The livery owner nodded and copped another hit for his trouble.

'Yes!' he squealed. 'She took it just after dark.'

'Did she tell you what she wanted it for?'

'Yes. She said she was goin' to bust Swift out.'

'Did she happen to say where she was going afterward?' Lawson sneered.

'No.'

Whack.

'No, honest.'

Lawson then looked at Laredo.

We know for sure now that it was her, but we still don't know where they went.'

'What about the mine?' Mossop pointed out.

'You saw the blood he left behind. He wouldn't have made the ride out there. No, he's close.'

Lawson dropped his gaze to the livery owner.

'Get out,' he snapped.

The frightened man scrambled to his feet and fled through the door. Mossop started to follow him.

'Where are you goin', Laredo?' Lawson asked him.

'To tear the damn town apart,' Laredo snarled. 'If he's here, I'll find him.'

★   ★   ★

Itza-chu knew something was wrong the instant a covey of quail was flushed from the brush on the other side of the wash. How the intruder had managed to get so close bewildered him. At first, he thought that it must be another Apache but then he dismissed the idea. If it was an Apache, he would have come in when he saw Itza-chu.

The sun was still reasonably high in the western sky; there were still a few hours until sundown. He walked slowly towards a large rock where his Winchester leaned against the rough surface, trying not to arouse suspicion.

Every step brought him closer to his rifle, but the distance, though closing, felt like an eternity. The Apache cursed himself for being so careless, knowing deep down that it could very well cost him his life.

Itza-chu reached out with his left hand to pick up the Winchester. No sooner had his fingertips touched it than the flat report of a rifle rang out, echoing across the desert. An audible *thwack* sounded as the bullet smashed into the Apache's back, shoving him violently forward.

The force of the blow knocked all of the air from his lungs. For several minutes he lay in the dirt, gasping for breath. Time passed slowly for what seemed an age, until a large shadow fell across Itza-chu's prone form.

Slowly the wounded Apache rolled on to his back and looked up at the large dark-skinned man who stood over him. Murphy spat in the dust.

'Who said you can't out Apache an Apache.'

With a thin trickle of blood running from the corner of his mouth and a low gurgle emanating from within his chest, Itza-chu opened his mouth to speak, revealing bloodstained teeth. At first, nothing came out, but he tried again. Instead of speaking, the Apache started to sing his own death song.

Murphy raised the .56 caliber Spencer and placed it against the Apache's forehead.

'Say hello to Cochise for me.'

The report of yet another gunshot rolled across the desert. The impact of the slug caused Itza-chu's head to bounce against the hard-packed earth. Murphy looked down at the dead Indian, satisfied that his work here was done. Now he could go back into town and collect his money. First, though, he needed something over which to sling the body.

Then he spotted Rosie.

Twenty minutes later, the large Negro had the Apache's body draped over the back of the mule, ready to head to Big Springs.

I didn't know it at the time, but my list of men to kill had just increased by one.

11

It seemed to be a growing habit, waking up with a pretty young woman taking care of me. However, as pain radiated from my side, I decided that it was one that I didn't want to get used to.

When I awoke I was on a lumpy mattress on a makeshift wooden cot. It was set up inside a single-room cabin with a hard-packed earthen floor; thin planks lined the walls and a stretched canvas formed a crude roof. The room was dim as a rag was draped over the single window hole; a small lantern lit the interior of the cabin.

Moaning as I came awake, I lifted my left arm to rub my face. Immediately I wished I hadn't. A sharp pain ripped through my side and caused me to gasp.

'Take it easy, Billy,' Casey ordered me firmly. 'You're a little the worse for wear this time around.'

I managed to pry an eye open. I looked up at my nurse.

'This is becoming a habit.'

'A pleasant one, I would hope.'

'If I have to get shot each time to have you standing over my bed then I may pass the next time,' I said drily. 'It damn well hurts.'

She laughed softly.

'Where am I?'

'Malachi's claim,' Casey said.

'Who?'

'It's mine,' a high-pitched croaky voice said.

I turned my head and saw an older man with worn clothes and gray hair sitting on a chair by a ramshackle table.

'Who are you?'

'The girl just told you who I was, son,' he said in a gruff voice. 'I ain't goin' to repeat it for the likes of you.'

'Never mind him,' Casey said to me. 'He's grumpy most of the time and plain angry the rest of it.'

I smiled.

'And if you didn't do what you done then you wouldn't be in the fix you're in,' he growled.

'Malachi was a friend of my father,' she explained. I nodded and looked at him.

'Thanks for takin' me in.'

'I didn't do it for you. I did it for her.'

'Ignore him,' Casey said. Malachi stood up from the chair.

'Don't bother me none,' he said. 'I'll just go on outside and watch the cactus grow.'

'Are you hungry?' Casey asked me after the door had shut behind him.

'I could eat,' I told her. 'What time is it?'

'It's afternoon.'

'OK.'

'How did I get here? Where *is* here?'

'We're out near Empty Springs. We got here on your horse.'

'I see,' I muttered, trying to work how far it was to the mine.

'Malachi took the bullet out of you, then I did the rest. There is no infection but you did have a temperature the first day. A few more days rest and you should be good.'

Then I remembered Itza-chu and Washington Murphy. *Hell!* I made to get up.

'I ain't got a few days. I need to get out to the mine.'

'You can't go anywhere; you won't make it two miles before you fall out of the saddle.'

'You don't understand,' I said to her, trying to remove her hand from my chest. 'There is a feller headed out to the mine to kill someone there.'

'The Apache?'

'Yeah. I gotta try to help him.'

She shook her head.

'Let me up, Casey,' I ordered her. 'I'm goin'.'

'You don't understand, Billy,' she said. 'You can't help him. You've been here two days.'

At first I was shocked. Two days? Then I gathered myself and used all the strength I had to climb out of bed. Big mistake! The room started to spin, the pain in my side stabbed deep, then things started to go black.

I passed out.

★ ★ ★

When I awoke from my dark dreams, it was also dark outside. Over flaming Colts I'd been killing men that I'd forgotten existed. Everything came down to the last one: Laredo Mossop. His laughing face haunted my dreams as he fired shot after shot into my body.

I lay there listening to the noises that filtered into the shack from outside. I became aware of Casey sitting in a chair beside me. When I moved she came alert.

'You're awake again,' she said softly.

'Yeah. I guess I should have listened to you.' I felt sheepish. 'How long was I out for?'

'It's a little after midnight,' she told me. 'Are you hungry? There is some soup I've kept warm just in case you woke up.'

A wave of weariness swept over me.

'Sounds good, Casey, but I think I need more sleep.'

I felt her hand touch my arm as I drifted once more into darkness.

★   ★   ★

The following morning, while I slept, the giant bounty hunter, Washington Murphy, rode into Big Springs with the decomposing corpse of Itza-chu draped over Rosie. He eased his horse to a stop in front of the jail and dismounted.

Lawson and Laredo Mossop walked out on to the boardwalk and caught a whiff of the rank odor emanating from the putrefying load.

'Did you have to bring the damned thing here?' Lawson complained, screwing his nose up.

'I want my money,' Murphy grunted.

'I can't give it to you,' Lawson said. 'I'll need to send a wire to the nearest fort and then they'll fix it from their end. Once they clear the funds I'd say you'll be able to get your money from the bank.'

The bounty hunter stared at Lawson. His gaze sent a chill down the hardened gunman's spine. Murphy grunted again and gathered the reins of his horse. He turned and had started to walk away when Lawson called after him.

'Where the hell are you goin'? You can't leave the damned thing here.'

Murphy turned, looked at the corpse and then at Lawson.

'I'll be in the saloon,' he said. He kept walking.

Lawson turned his gaze to Laredo, who shrugged his shoulders and walked back inside the jail.

'Hell!' Lawson cursed. He stomped down the steps and led the mule away.

'Is that the Indian who was out at the mine?' Jones called out as he approached along the street.

'Yeah.'

Jones stopped beside his hired man.

'Good. I'll send a couple of men out there to sit tight until we find Swift.'

'I'd send more than a couple out there.'

'I thought you said he was wounded?'

'I did.' Lawson nodded. 'But if we don't find him before he's fit enough, then he'll be a handful once again.'

'Well you'd better find him — soon,' Jones snapped; then he looked at the body on the mule. 'I have an idea.'

'Uh-huh.'

'Has our friend Murphy left town yet?'

'Nope. He's waitin' on his reward money. Said I could find him in the saloon,' Lawson told him.

'Good.' A cold smile split Jones's face. 'I think I'm going to put him to work while he's here.'

Lawson looked about.

'If you mean by lookin' for Swift, then don't mention it around Mossop. He's got a burr under his saddle as it is without anyone else stompin' on his corns.'

'I don't care.' Jones snorted. 'I want that bastard caught before anything else happens.'

Lawson watched as he stormed off. He couldn't help but feel that things were getting out of hand.

* * *

Jones found Murphy sitting at a scarred table in a dark corner of the saloon working on a bottle of rye. He dragged a chair over and sat down. Murphy gave him a cold look.

'What do you want?' he asked.

'I want to offer you a chance to make some more money,' Jones offered.

Murphy sat the half-empty glass down on the table with a clunk.

'I'm listenin'.'

Jones went on to tell him about me and the problems I had been causing while they tried to get me out of the picture.

'I'm offering two thousand dollars to find him,' Jones said. 'I don't care if he's dead or alive, I just want him gone.'

Murphy thought about the offer and shook his head.

'More money,' he said.

Jones opened his mouth to protest, then dismissed the idea.

'Three thousand dollars?'

'OK.'

'One more thing,' Jones added. 'Watch your step around Laredo Mossop. He wants Swift too. Maybe more than me.'

Murphy gave Jones a dark look.

'If he gets in the way I'll kill him too.'

★ ★ ★

Over the next two days, I grew better and stronger, though I worried about the mine. On the second day Casey suggested that Malachi should go to town to see if there was any news. I protested against this idea at first, but he needed supplies so he had to go anyway.

Big Springs was a half-day ride westward; he left the following morning. While he was gone, I continued to improve, finding that I could walk around virtually pain free. Who wouldn't get better with all the food Casey was feeding me?

When Malachi arrived back at the claim the following afternoon he did so with the look of a man who had trouble piled high on his shoulders. He sat at the table and began to tell me what was happening in Big Springs. I didn't like it one bit.

'The Apache who was out at your mine was brought in over the back of a mule by the bounty hunter, Murphy,' he explained. 'They know that Casey was involved with your escape and they've been turnin' the town upside down to find you. Word has it that Jones has offered Murphy three thousand dollars to find you. So, between him and Laredo Mossop, the folks have had a tough time. The town doctor, Obadiah Peters, was beat up tryin' to get information outta him 'cause they know you were wounded. Mossop done that.'

The more he told me the more concerned I grew.

'Also,' Malachi concluded, 'Jones sent three men out to your mine to sit on it, just in case you showed up there.'

'Oh, Billy.' Casey sighed. 'What are you going to do?'

I got up from the table and walked over to where my Peacemakers were hanging. I took them down, strapped them on and tied the thongs about my thighs.

'Did you get me some cartridges while you were in town?' I asked Malachi.

'Two boxes for each,' he confirmed. I nodded.

'I'll be needin' them.'

'What are you going to do?' Casey asked again while Malachi went to get me the ammunition.

'First I'm takin' back the mine, then I'm goin' to town,' I told her. 'I got me

143

some men to kill.'

'But you're still — '

'I'm fit enough to kill them bastards,' I snapped, then immediately wished I hadn't. 'I'm sorry. But Jones has killed the only person that meant anythin' to me and he deserves to pay for it. The others have it comin', too.'

'What about me?' Casey cried. 'Don't I mean anything to you?'

I could see the moisture form in her green eyes and I felt a feeling like no other. At that very moment I considered walking away from what I was about to do and asking her to come with me. I could still feel the kiss that we'd shared in the jail cell and I wanted to take her in my arms and kiss her again. Tell her that everything would be all right; but I knew that I could be dead within the week.

'Yes, you do,' I said, my response measured. 'But this is something I have to see through to the end.'

'It doesn't mean I agree with it.'

144

I reached up and wiped a tear from her cheek.

'I'll be back.'

Malachi came back with the boxes of cartridges and gave them to me.

'Take care of Casey,' I told him.

He just nodded.

I looked at Casey again.

'I'll be fine,' I said, hoping to reassure her.

'Let me get you some food then,' she offered.

'OK,' I said.

Twenty minutes later I rode off into the darkness on my buckskin, headed for the mine. It was time to put things right.

12

The three men whom Jones had sent to the mine were working it. Well, two were, while the other man remained on watch. I lay belly down at the crest of a small hill on the other side of the wash, watching them while the afternoon sun sank slowly toward the horizon.

My plan was to wait until dark and then move in on foot. I wanted to keep at least one of them alive to go back to Jones and deliver a message.

I waited patiently until the last rays of the afternoon sun faded and night was settling across the desert. I left the buckskin where it was and moved in. I navigated through the cactus and surrounding brush, down through the wash and up the other side.

They were all seated at the fire eating beans and bacon for supper when I came upon them. I held my Winchester at waist height, cocked and ready to fire.

'You fellers are trespassin',' I told them.

When they saw me there was a scramble for guns. Plates of food went flying as their panic set in.

My Winchester roared; the man on the far right was thrust back by an invisible force before he could bring his rifle to bear. The second man had his six-gun level when I switched my aim. I levered another cartridge into the breech as I did so.

The man's six-gun bucked in his hand and I felt the slug pass close. The Winchester in my hands thundered again and the slug took the shooter through his right lung. The third man hesitated and realized his mistake too late. By that time I'd levered another round and had time to place my next shot where I wanted it.

The .45-.70 slug slammed into his shoulder, spinning him around. He fell to the ground next to his fallen friends, writing as the pain started to flood his body. I hurried over to them and kicked their weapons out of reach. Then I bent and checked all three men.

The first man I'd shot was dead. There was no doubt there, the bullet had blown his brains across the desert. The second man was gurgling as he slowly drowned in his own blood. I guessed he wouldn't see the next ten minutes out.

The man I'd wounded was moaning in pain. When I stood over him, he looked up at me and cursed.

'You damned low-down skunk, you shot me,' he gasped.

'You three were tryin' your best to do the same to me,' I pointed out. 'Now, get up.'

'I can't,' he moaned. 'I'm shot, damn it.'

Leaning down I took a fistful of his collar and dragged him to his feet.

'Hey! *Ouch*! Be careful,' he cried out in protest.

'Get over to your horses,' I said once

he was on his feet.

'Why?'

'Because you're ridin' back to Big Springs to give Jones a message for me.'

'But I got a slug in me.'

'Then you'll have to see the doctor when you get there. But you're goin', and that's it.'

'The hell I am! I won't make it.'

I took out one of my Peacemakers and held it in a threatening gesture. His eyes grew wide.

'Are you goin' to shoot me now? Is that it?'

Behind me, the dying man's gurgles grew louder. I turned and shot him in the head, putting an end to his slow death.

'What the hell did you do that for?'

I turned to the man I'd shot in the shoulder. I placed the hard barrel against his forehead.

'What's your name?'

'Chris.' He cringed. 'Why?'

'I wanted to know so I could put the name on your grave marker.'

'Whoa! OK, I'll go.'

'Damn right you will!' I scowled and lowered the Peacemaker. 'Now get over to the horses.'

I put a saddle on a bay while Chris stood by and moaned about his wound. I made sure he had water and helped him mount.

'How am I goin' to get off by myself?' he whined. I shrugged.

'Don't get off.' I gave him his reins. 'Tell Jones I'm comin' for him. Tell him to expect me. And tell Laredo Mossop I'm goin' to bury him like his brothers.'

'But — '

Yelling loudly I slapped the horse on the rump. It lunged forward and took off into the night. In the morning I would get rid of the bodies and head back to Malachi's claim. From there I would set in motion the next part of my plan.

But things had happened while I was gone that I wouldn't learn of until my return. Once again, everything would change.

★ ★ ★

Malachi's howls of pain brought Casey running from inside the mining shack. He lay in the gravel half-way up the slope to his diggings grasping at his leg. She clambered up the slope and knelt beside him.

'Oh, Lord. What happened?'

'Fell over my own dang feet,' he said through gritted teeth. 'I think I done broke my leg, girl.'

'Let me have a look.'

Casey examined Malachi's left leg and didn't like the look of it.

'I need to get you into the shack, Malachi. And then I need to go to Big Springs for the doctor.'

'Damn foolish girl,' Malachi admonished her. 'They'll be watchin' for you. You'll be ridin' into the bear's den.'

'What else can I do? Billy has been gone three days. Even if he comes back it'll still be at least that many before he gets here.'

'Dang it, Casey . . . '

151

'Malachi, if Doc Peters doesn't look at that leg, you could lose it or even die.'

He nodded because he knew she was right.

'All right, girl. Get me into the shack and go.'

It took ten minutes to get the injured man back to his shack and another ten or so to saddle the horse he used. When Casey was ready to leave she checked on him and made sure everything he required was within reach. That included an old Colt Navy model that he carried occasionally.

'You be careful, Casey,' he cautioned her. 'It'll be dark when you get there, but don't take no chances.'

'You worry too much,' she assured him. 'I'll be back tomorrow. Don't go anywhere.'

Not until after she'd walked out did he realize what she'd said.

'As if I'm goin' anywhere,' he grumbled.

He listened to the sound of receding hoofbeats.

★   ★   ★

Casey reached Big Springs an hour before midnight. She circled around the town and came in so that she wouldn't have to ride past the jail and the assay office. The part of town where Doc Peters lived was dimly lit, so she felt sure she could reach there unnoticed.

All was quiet. There were few lit windows as much of the town was sleeping and most buildings were blacked out. When Casey reached the doctor's home she saw a faint light through a gap in a curtain. She tied the horse to the fence, hurried up the front steps and strode across the veranda to the front door.

Casey knocked urgently on the paneled timber, waited briefly, then knocked again. She heard footsteps on the floorboards inside, then the lock snicked and the door swung open. The lean, gray-haired Obadiah Peters answered the door.

'Casey, what . . . ?'

She didn't give him time to say more as she pushed past him and into he hallway.

'I need your help, Obadiah,' she pleaded. 'Malachi has broken his . . . '

She paused and peered intently at his face. Even though the lamplight was dim she could still see the marks from the beating he'd received.

'Oh no!' she blurted out. 'What did they do to you? I'm sorry you've been caught up in this.'

He ignored her apology. 'What are you doing here, Casey? If they find you here . . . '

'Malachi has broken his leg. He's out at his shack. You need to look at it.'

Peters thought for a moment as his mind whirled with what Casey had told him.

'OK. Meet me outside of town near the large triple cactus. Do you know where I mean?'

Casey nodded. 'Sure. I think I know it.'

'Good, I'll be there as soon as I've collected a few things.'

Peters ushered her out of his house and closed the door. Casey climbed on to the horse and rode back out of town.

★   ★   ★

Casey waited almost half an hour before she heard the approach of the doctor's small buggy. He stopped the vehicle beside her.

'I'm sorry I took so long,' he said. 'There was something I had to do.'

Before she could speak a new voice spoke up.

'Yeah, he had to get me.'

Lawson emerged from the darkness with a six-gun in his fist. As soon as she saw him Casey made to set her horse running but she wasn't quick enough. Lawson dragged her from the saddle and she landed on the hard-packed ground with a solid bump.

155

'Let go of me, you animal!' she cried out, struggling to break free of his grasp.

Lawson dragged her to her feet and shook her, still using only one hand.

'Just you settle down, missy, or you're likely to get hurt.'

She looked at Peters.

'Why?' she screamed at him. 'Malachi could die because of you.'

Casey tried to break free of Lawson but he holstered his six-gun, then slapped her across her face.

'I warned you.'

She stopped struggling, stunned by the force of the blow.

'I'm sorry,' she heard Peters say. 'But they said they would hurt Mary if I helped any of you and they found out.'

'And a great help you were too,' Lawson gloated.

'He'll come for me and he'll kill you,' Casey spat at Lawson.

'Who? Lightning?'

'Yes, Lightning,' she shouted.

'Where is he,' came a deep voice

from the darkness.

Casey's head turned quickly and she saw a large man emerge from the gloom.

'Yeah, where is he? Is he out at the old man's claim? Malachi, was that his name?' Lawson asked.

'You stay away from him,' she hissed. 'He's hurt.'

Lawson looked at the large man; it was Murphy.

'Why don't you go and check it out. Where is he, Doc?'

'Don't you tell him, Obadiah,' Casey snapped.

'Doc?'

'Out near Empty Springs,' Peters told him with a heavy sigh. 'You can't miss it.'

'Leave him alone, you bastard,' Casey screamed. She broke into a fresh bout of struggling. Lawson clipped her on the chin with a clenched fist and she collapsed into his arms. He turned to say something to Murphy but the big man was already gone.

★ ★ ★

The next day, around mid-afternoon, Malachi heard a horse approaching. He was feverish and the pain from his broken leg had got worse. The horse stopped outside the shack and the rider dismounted. Footfalls on gravel gave off a crunching sound.

'Casey? Is that you?' he called out.

The footfalls came closer.

'Casey?'

Still no answer.

With a trembling hand, Malachi reached for the Navy Colt. No sooner had his hand wrapped around its grips than a huge figure, silhouetted by bright sunlight, filled the doorway. Malachi froze.

'Who are you?'

'Hello, old man.' A deep voice filled the shack. 'You and me need to have a talk.'

As the big man approached the bed Malachi tried frantically to bring up the heavy six-gun and hold it steady

158

enough to fire. The attempt, however, was futile and the bounty hunter known as Washington Murphy was on him before he managed to fire.

13

When the wounded man named Chris finally reached Big Springs his shoulder was a putrefying mess and the infection had spread throughout his body. He was a dead man riding. How he'd stayed in the saddle so long was anyone's guess, let alone found his way to town. His horse trudged slowly along the main street towards the jail.

The dying man swayed left and right in the saddle with the rolling gait of his horse. He mumbled words and every now and then a loud outburst would escape his lips.

The townsfolk stopped to stare as he passed by. No one moved to help him. They all knew who he was and what he'd been doing. Well, it looked to them as though he'd poked the bear and the bear had all but killed him. Served him right, some would say later, out of earshot.

The half-dead rider made it as far as the jail, where the horse stopped facing the hitch rail. Neither it nor its rider moved, they just stayed there.

Suddenly the rider shouted hoarsely: 'Watch out! He's behind us.'

The door to the jail opened and three men came outside. Lawson, Jones and Laredo stood on the boardwalk and stared at the solitary figure.

'Is that . . . ?' started Jones.

'Yeah,' answered Lawson. 'It's one of the men you sent out to the mine.'

Laredo stared quietly at the rider.

'Is he dead?'

Lawson stepped down from the boardwalk and out into the street. He walked over to the dust-caked horse and looked up at the rider. It was immediately evident by the the sickly scent of putrefaction that the man was all but dead; he screwed up his nose. He noticed that Chris's gunbelt was looped over the saddle horn to keep him in the saddle. His face was gaunt, his cheeks sunken and sallow.

Lawson shoved him, looking for a reaction. The half-dead rider cracked open his eyes and looked down at him.

'He killed us,' Chris mumbled through parched lips. 'He came out of the . . . '

Chris's voice caught in his throat as he coughed. He started to speak again; this time his voice was more a dry rasp.

'He came out of the dark and shot us all,' he said. 'Wanted . . . wanted me to give a message to . . . to Jones.'

'What did he say?'

'He said to tell Jones he was comin',' Chris gasped. 'And . . . and to tell Mossop he was goin' to bury . . . bury him like his brothers.'

After he'd finished the sentence Chris fell silent. For a moment Lawson thought he'd passed out. He gave him a gentle push but nothing happened.

'Hey, Chris.'

Nothing. Lawson realized that the rider wasn't breathing. He'd lived long enough to deliver the message, then he'd died.

'Damn it!' Lawson muttered, turning away from the stinking corpse. 'This feller is becoming more trouble than he's worth.'

'What happened,' Jones called down to him.

'Swift turned up at the claim and killed the others there,' Lawson explained as he stomped up on to the boardwalk. 'He let Chris go because he wanted to send a message.'

'Damn it!' Laredo Mossop cursed. 'I'm goin' after him.'

'You don't need to,' Lawson told him. 'He's comin' here. That was the message.'

'I sure wish he'd hurry up,' Laredo grumbled. 'I'm sick of waitin' for him. I want him dead and buried.'

'If you ain't noticed, that seems to be a bit of a problem at the moment. Everyone who's gone up against him is dead. Includin' your brothers — and he has plans of plantin' you beside them.'

'I'd best watch my back then,' Laredo said arrogantly. 'There ain't no way he could kill me by facin' me.'

He spun on his heel and walked back inside.

'Is he that good?' Jones asked.

'Maybe. It was said once that there wasn't as much as a cigarette paper between him and Lightning back when he was burnin' them down,' Lawson told Jones. 'And yeah, Lightning has been out of the action for a time but I doubt he's lost all of his gun speed. He was a natural when it came down to it, so if I was Laredo I'd tread warily.'

'And if it came down to a gunfight between the two of them?'

'If you'd asked me before today, I would have backed Laredo every time. But now I don't know.'

'What about you?' Jones asked. 'If you remember, when this all started I hired you for the job.'

Lawson spat on the boardwalk.

'Hell, if I get half a chance I'll backshoot the sonuver.'

* * *

As I drew closer to Malachi's mining shack the sun was an hour from going down. The desert was starting to change colors as the giant yellow orb descended slowly. My horse picked its way between the clumps of cactus and rock as I took in the strangely comforting landscape. I was looking forward to seeing Casey, eating a hot meal, and a good night's sleep. All in that order.

My stomach rumbled at the thought of Casey's cooking and when I topped a low hill the shack came into view. I drew rein that instant, as it was obvious that something wasn't right. There was no movement, no wood smoke from a cook fire outside the shack, and Malachi's horse was gone.

Leaning forward, I took the Winchester from its scabbard and worked the lever. I waited for a minute or two and scanned the area, looking for anything out of place. Still nothing moved.

165

The buckskin moved forward after a gentle nudge with my heels. I rested the butt of the rifle on my thigh, my finger alongside the trigger. I rocked with the horse's motion as it moved down the hill and across the littered ground, closing the distance. If anyone was there, whether friendly or otherwise, I couldn't tell. However, years of living by the gun gave me a sixth sense for trouble. And right now it was screaming at me.

I caught a flicker of movement at the rag used for a curtain. It was only a hint of a flutter, as though a breeze had touched it.

There was no breeze.

I dived from the saddle as a rifle poking from a slim gap roared into life. The bullet that sped from its barrel passed through the space where I'd been only a heartbeat before. The jarring spasm that I felt when I hit the hard-packed ground caused me to gasp in agony as pain from my side tore through me.

Another shot rang out. With gritted teeth I crawled my way to the cover of a small crop of jagged rocks. Problem was that I wasn't the only occupant. A large diamondback rattler, as thick as my arm and twice as long, set his rattle whirring, warning of his imminent strike.

'Son of a . . . ' I rolled away with all speed in the opposite direction in time to avoid the strike range of the serpent.

However, that put me back out in the open again. More gunshots from the shack rang out, causing small eruptions of dirt to spurt about me. A sharp crack sounded as a slug passed close to my head. I came up to one knee and fired at the shack, the Winchester kicking back into my shoulder as it thundered. I saw the bullet chew splinters from the window frame. I fired again. This time the rag at the window flicked as the slug passed through it.

This brought forth another torrent of gunfire, which forced me to scramble behind a clump of cactus. More bullets whacked into the tubular stems of the plant I was behind and, not meeting resistance, they tunneled through easily.

Off to my left was a shallow wash, so I crawled over to it and slid down the embankment. Once at the bottom, I kept low and crossed to the other side. I peered over the edge and studied the shack. The rifleman fired again and an explosion of dirt and grit peppered my face. Whoever was inside was a reasonable shot.

Brushing the grit from my face, I moved a little way along the wash and crept up the bank again. I slid the Winchester up over the lip and sighted along the barrel. Then I paused. There was no way I could get at whoever was inside without exposing myself. So I decided to wait until dark.

Or I thought I would.

'Are you still alive, Lightning Swift?' a deep voice called out across the desert void. A man's voice.

When he received no answer he called out again.

'I do not believe you are dead. Maybe you are pretending.'

'What do you want?' I called back.

'You!'

'Where are the others?'

'The old man is here,' he answered. 'The girl is in town. The sheriff has her.'

A million thoughts ran through my mind.

'Did you hear me?' he called out.

'I heard you.'

'You will come out or I will shoot the old man,' he ordered.

I heard faint voices come from inside the shack.

'Are you Murphy?' I asked.

'Yeah.'

'How do I know that Malachi ain't already dead?'

A high-pitched scream came from inside.

'Does that answer your question?'

It did. I formulated a plan in my mind. It wasn't elaborate and might get me killed but I was sure Murphy would kill me anyway. If he didn't, then someone else would. Once again, like days of old, I would have to rely on gun speed.

'What's to say that if I come out you won't shoot me down cold?' I shouted to him.

'That's a chance you'll have to take,' Murphy called back. 'Jones said he'd pay three thousand dollars for me to find you. He didn't care if you were dead or alive. I can kill you here or I can take you in. Your choice.'

Tucking my right side Colt into the back of my pants, I stood up. I raised my hands in the air; the right one held the rifle out to the side. The way I was standing hid my empty holster, and I made sure that the bounty hunter couldn't see it.

'I'm comin' out, Murphy,' I yelled.

'Don't come any closer until you get rid of your guns.'

I dropped the Winchester to the ground, followed by my twin holsters.

'All right, come ahead.'

170

Slowly I walked towards the shack. My body tensed as I expected a bullet to tear into my flesh at any moment. Ahead of me I saw Murphy emerge from the shack, rifle in his hands. As I'd heard, he was a big man with dark skin. Instead of a broad-brimmed hat he wore a forage cap. In his large hands, a 7-shot Spencer was held ready to fire.

There were ten yards between us when I stopped. The Colt tucked into my pants at the back felt as though it was there for all the world to see.

'So you're the great Lightning Swift,' Murphy sneered.

'That was a long time ago,' I told him. Then I asked, 'What's wrong with Malachi?'

'The old man?' Murphy asked in a deep voice.

'Yeah.' I nodded.

A large smile split his face, revealing teeth that seemed whiter than normal against the darkness of his skin.

'Nothing now.'

I grew cold inside. All Malachi had done was give us shelter. He didn't deserve to be murdered. I knew my fate was sealed if I didn't act.

'I guess that proves it then,' I said, holding my emotions in check.

'What?'

'On the outside, you may be black, but on the inside you're all Apache.'

His was a hate that simmered just below the surface. Suddenly it exploded to the surface, as I'd hoped. He started to swing the Spencer up to shoot me but I was already moving. To me, it felt slow and labored. The Spencer whip-lashed and by luck the shot missed. The next one wouldn't.

My hand was behind my back, clamped round the Peacemaker's grips. It came clear of my pants and I brought it into view. Murphy's eyes grew wide when he realized he was in trouble. The Peacemaker came up level with its hammer on full cock.

The big bounty hunter was about to squeeze the trigger again when my Colt slammed a shot into his barrel-sized chest. Murphy took a half-step backward as the slug buried deep but he refused to go down. He let out a wild snarl like a wounded beast.

My Peacemaker bucked again. The .45 slug smashed into his breastbone, splintering it, sending razor-sharp shards slicing into his lungs. Still he refused to fall. My mind flashed back to Harley Mossop.

With all the strength he could muster Washington Murphy lined the Spencer up on my chest and smiled. His teeth were now red with blood as it bubbled up from his damaged lungs. He spat a red globule at me.

'Now I'll kill you,' he snarled.

'Not this time, you big son of a bitch,' I declared. The Peacemaker bucked a third time.

The big bounty hunter's head snapped back as the slug punched into his forehead, extinguishing his candle for good. He dropped the Spencer and fell like a giant cedar, crashing to the

173

ground and raised a small cloud of dust.

'You won't be murderin' anyone ever again,' I said aloud as I stared down at his unmoving form.

14

Malachi was on the floor when I found him. He lay on his back, eyes staring sightlessly at the canvas ceiling. He'd been beaten some and had visible cuts and bruises on his face. My eyes drifted to the bloody stain on his shirt where Murphy's large-bladed knife had sliced through it and carved deep into his chest.

Bastard!

I walked back outside and looked about for a pick. Before I rode on to Big Springs I would give the old miner the burial he deserved.

It took me an hour to dig a hole big enough and it was dark by the time I finished. I placed Malachi gently into it, wrapped in a blanket from his bed. As I filled it in by the silvery light of a full moon, a coyote's high-pitched howls signaled the passing of another life in an already bloody saga.

Tomorrow I would ride to Big Springs and attempt to free Casey. After I'd seen her to safety, I would set about ridding the territory of the final three men I had yet to kill.

I spent most of the night tossing and turning on hard-packed earth outside the shack. Somehow it didn't seem right to use the bed of a dead man. Throughout the night the single coyote that I'd heard when burying Malachi was joined by more. The darkness was soon filled with their yips and howls. Attracted by the scent of the dead bounty hunter, they came in close and at one point I could see blue eyes as they glowed in the firelight.

To the east the morning dawned into a pale pink sky that crept overhead and devoured the few remaining stars, the last vestiges of the night. The coyotes were gone and the horses started to stir. I rose and prepared to ride for Big Springs.

By the time I'd packed a few things

and loaded the corpse of Murphy on to his horse the sun was well up. A lone buzzard circled high in the clear blue sky. The day was already hot but was bound to grow hotter. The body of the bounty hunter would be quite ripe by the time I hit town. Too bad.

Then a phrase from the Bible that I'd read a long time ago came to me:

And I looked, and behold a pale horse: and his name that sat on him was Death, and Hell followed with him.

My arrival in Big Springs was heralded by the barking of a dog from a narrow alley between the blacksmith's shop and the livery. I stopped the horses in the shadows and waited to see if the animal had aroused any suspicion.

It was after midnight and most of the town was quiet except for the saloon, which was still open and serving customers. The main street, however, was almost deserted and shrouded in shadows. I led the horses behind the livery and left them there while I broke in through the back door. Once inside I looked about until I found what I required: a coal-oil lantern and some matches.

I went back outside; I left my buckskin where it was and led the horse that carried Murphy's now stinking corpse along the back of the buildings until I figured I was level with the jail. That was where I left it. I continued walking to the assayer's office.

The coal-oil smell was strong as I emptied it from the lamp on to the tinder-dry plank wall. When it was empty I tossed it away and fished the matches from my pocket. I took one; after a couple of strikes it flared to life.

When the flame touched the coal oil, it spread up the wall. I stood back and watched to make sure it would burn. Very soon the back wall was consumed by orange and blue flames. I smiled with satisfaction and jogged off to where I'd left Murphy's horse. There I waited.

★   ★   ★

Delbert Jones and Gray Lawson were in the saloon when I set fire to the assay office. Mossop was there too but, as usual, he sat by himself at a corner table brooding over a glass of whiskey.

'I'm surprised he's stuck around so long,' Jones observed, nodding at Laredo.

'While Swift is still alive he won't go anywhere,' Lawson told him. 'Hate runs deep in him.'

'Do you think he'll come?'

'While we have the girl he will,' Lawson said. 'That's if Laredo or the bounty hunter don't get him first.'

Lawson took out a sack of tobacco and fashioned himself a smoke. He placed it between his lips, moved it to one side and, as always, left it unlit.

'Why bother making one if you only do that with it?'

179

'It relaxes me.'

'*Fire!*'

Both men snapped their heads around to the saloon entrance. A tall thin man stood there with a panicked expression on his face.

'There's a fire. It's the assay office.'

Lawson leaped to his feet and cast the unlit smoke aside.

'Guess who's back?' he drawled as he headed for the doors.

Jones followed hot on his heels while Laredo Mossop remained seated, staring at his half-empty glass as if nothing had happened.

An orange glow filled the sky as they burst out on to the boardwalk. Without pausing they jumped to the street and continued running until they reached the assay office. It was well alight, the flames reaching high into the night sky. Loud cracks from the burning timber gave off a crackling sound.

From nowhere townsfolk started to gather and form a bucket brigade.

Water sloshed on to the hard-packed ground of the street as each vessel made its way along to be emptied on to the roaring flames.

It was a losing battle and Jones knew it. He stood by and could only watch as it all went up in smoke. There was a loud crash as part of the roof came down and a large plume of sparks billowed into the night sky. Shouts of volunteers echoed through the smoke-filled air as they worked tirelessly to save the buildings on either side of the assay office.

'It was him, wasn't it?' Jones said through gritted teeth.

'Most likely,' Lawson allowed. 'Just lettin' us know he was still around, I guess. I mean, why else would he burn your office to the ground?'

Jones's eyes opened wide as a thought flooded into his head.

'The girl,' he blurted out. 'He's come for the girl.'

Suddenly shots rang out from down the street.

I watched as the saloon emptied. A crowd gathered and made a vain attempt to save the assayer's office. When the street was clear I led the horse with Murphy's corpse draped over it and tied it to the hitch-rail. Hurriedly I climbed the steps and tried the door to the jail. It was locked.

Raising my leg, I made to kick it open when a voice snarled from the shadows.

'I been waitin' a long time for this.'

Without further thought I dived from the boardwalk and rolled. The gun in Laredo Mossop's fist barked twice and I felt the impacts as they thudded into the earth beside me. My right-side Peacemaker came free of the holster and I raised it to snap off a shot. It flew wide of the mark but not by much. I fired again and Laredo screamed. By some stroke of luck the slug from my Peacemaker had hit his six-gun.

He dropped it as though it was red

hot. Pain from the blow ran up his arm and into his shoulder, turning it numb. He grabbed at it with his left hand as his face screwed up in hatred and pain. Then he saw me rising to my feet and his hand dropped for his second gun.

'Don't,' I snapped loudly. 'I'll kill you now if you try.'

His hand froze just above the jutting gun butt. I could see in his face that it took all of his willpower not to pull the weapon.

'Our time will come,' I assured him. 'But first I got me things to do. But it will come.'

Shouts were coming from down the street and as I looked up I could see figures running towards us. I cursed inwardly because I knew I had to leave or be outgunned.

Backing away I kept looking at Laredo Mossop.

'Don't move. I'm goin' but I'll be back. If I see you followin' me I'll blow your damned head off.'

Laredo stood still and watched me

disappear down a darkened alley. As soon as I was out of sight I ran as hard as I could, fully expecting the darkness behind me to erupt in a blaze of gunfire. There was, however, nothing to hear but the pounding of my boots on the hard-packed earth.

When I reached my buckskin I leaped into the saddle, turned his head and kicked him hard to send him into a dead run across the desert.

★   ★   ★

'What the hell happened here?' Jones snarled as he approached Laredo Mossop. 'What was all that shooting?'

'That damned Swift was here,' Laredo answered in a menacing voice. 'While you two were playin' at puttin' that fire out, he was about to break into the jail. My guess is he was lookin' for the girl.'

'That's what we figured too,' Lawson said in agreement. Then his gaze drifted to the horse with the bounty hunter's body over it. 'Hell!'

'Is that . . . ?' Jones hesitated, 'Is that Murphy?'

Lawson walked up to the horse for a closer inspection and wished he hadn't. The sickly sweet smell was almost overpowering.

'Yeah, it's him,' he said with his hand over his mouth and nose.

Lawson saw Laredo rubbing at his arm.

'Are you OK?' he asked.

'Yeah, the bastard got lucky is all,' he grumbled. 'Shot the gun outta my hand. He said it ain't over, though. I'd say while you still got the girl you hold all the cards. He'll try rescuin' her again real soon.'

'That's it!' Jones exclaimed. 'Come mornin' we hire more men and see if we can draw him out. We'll use the girl as bait.'

'Don't go hirin' no cow nurses to do the job you want done,' Laredo warned Jones. 'They'll only get in my way when the time comes. If they do, I'll blow

185

them to hell and gone too.'

'I don't care,' Jones shot back. 'I want this done before we have the damned marshals climbing all over this damned town.'

He turned his gaze back to Lawson.

'Send a man out in the morning to see if they can find him. I don't care who. Offer him a hundred dollars to find Swift and tell him to be in town by mid-afternoon tomorrow. If he ain't, he'll never see the girl again. Tell him I'll bury her in a mine.'

★   ★   ★

I spent the rest of the night in a deep wash about a mile from town. When the sun came up I found a piece of high ground where I could watch the town. Although the bulk of the fire was out it still smoldered and a brown stain of woodsmoke hung lazily above the town. The morning was crisp and the sky cloudless. Another hot desert day.

At the moment I was at a loss as to

186

what to do next. Somehow I had to get Casey back without getting myself killed — and now they would be expecting me.

I moved from the high ground back to the wash to try and figure out my next move. I was still there when I heard the noise of an approaching horse. Swiftly I drew a Colt and scrambled up to the lip of the wash. I was in time to see a man around one hundred yards away following my sign. I cursed my carelessness.

I slid back down the slope and changed my position so I could come up behind the rider when he reached the wash. A short time later I did just that.

'Hold it there!' I snapped, aiming my Peacemaker at his midriff. 'Why are you bird-doggin' my trail?'

He swung his bay horse around. Once he saw my six-gun he raised his hands.

'Easy there, pilgrim,' he drawled. 'A feller called Jones offered a hundred dollars for someone to come out here and find you to deliver a message.'

'What's the message?'

'He says that if you don't come to town by mid-afternoon you won't ever see the girl again.'

I stared at him in silence. He looked to be in his mid-thirties and from the looks of his clothes he'd been around a bit.

'Just so you know,' he added, 'I don't agree with whatever he's got planned but I need that money, mister. Hell, for that much money I woulda delivered the message to ol' Lucifer hisself.'

'What's your name?'

'Chuck.'

'How would you like to earn some more money, Chuck?' I asked him. His eyes gave away his need.

'Doin' what?'

'I'll give you twenty dollars if you tell me all you know about what they got planned in town.'

He looked about nervously.

'Ride down into the wash and we'll

talk,' I told him.

'OK,' he agreed. He rode the bay over the lip and down on to the flat base of the wash, where he dismounted. I holstered my six-gun.

'All right, Chuck,' I said, 'tell me what you know.'

'I don't know a lot,' he replied. 'And I don't know if it will help you any, but that Jones feller was hirin' himself some more help this mornin'. I heard 'em talk about usin' the girl as bait. I don't abide that. Where I come from in Texas we treat our women with respect. But like I said, I needed the money.'

'I ain't goin' to hold that against you, Chuck,' I said. 'Just keep goin'. How were they goin' to use Casey?'

'That's her name?'

'Yeah.'

'They were goin' to set her out in the middle of the street with a couple of fellers ridin' herd on her,' he explained. 'I heard them say that they were goin' to turn that gunfighter, Mossop, loose on you. Seems he don't like you much.

189

I don't know why and I didn't ask. Anyhow, if you were to kill him then they were goin' to have a couple of fellers set up to bushwhack you. You can't win buckin' a stacked deck like that.'

I thought in silence for a long minute before I turned my attention back to Chuck.

'How would you like to earn some more money, Chuck?'

'Doin' what exactly?'

'When I come to town later and if I manage to get Casey free of them killers, can I count on you to get her away from here?'

'I g-guess so,' he said hesitantly.

I reached into my left pocket, took out $120 and gave it to him.

'You've made some good money today. I've got a mine, three days' ride from here. You take her there. You wait for another two days. If I ain't there on the third day you take Casey and get the hell out. Take her to Texas or wherever, but get her away. Don't hang around the mine because they'll come and kill both of you.'

'I can do that, Lightning.' Chuck nodded stoically.

'My friends call me Billy.' I stuck out my hand. He smiled.

'Sure, Billy.'

'You'd best head on back then,' I said. 'Circle the town and come in from the opposite direction. One other thing, when you get out of town don't wait for me. Like I said, go to the mine and wait there. If they catch me you'll be of no help. I'll be dead anyway.'

He nodded. 'Sure.'

'Thanks, Chuck,' I said when he was mounted on his bay. 'I'll see you out at the mine.'

'This might be a fool question, but where is it?'

'Just head straight for the Ajo Mountains. You'll find it.'

He rode back to Big Springs then and I watched him as he went, circling around the town and coming in on the other side as I'd instructed.

All I had to do now was get inside the town myself and release Casey from her captors.

15

Delbert Jones paced back and forth across the jail checking his pocket watch every five minutes and grumbling about how slowly time was moving. At last he took one final look.

'It's time, he said.'

Lawson took the keys down from their hook and walked over to the cell where Casey was housed. She was rather disheveled but was determined to carry herself with pride. Even after the failed attempt to free her the night before.

The key rattled in the lock and the door screeched in protest as it swung open. Casey sat on the cot and didn't move.

'Come on, out,' Lawson ordered.

She remained where she was.

'If I have to come in there, girl, I'll grab that pretty hair of yours and drag you out by it, damned if I won't.'

Slowly she rose to her feet and walked towards the cell door.

'Where are we going?' she asked hesitantly.

'Outside,' was all Lawson told her.

They walked outside and on to the street where two men waited. Both men were armed with rifles; Casey had never seen either of them before. Lawson stepped off to one side while Jones stood on the other. Laredo Mossop remained in the shade of the jail's awning, an almost uncaring expression upon his face. Three more men were placed strategically in the alleyways along the street. There were eight men in total.

The afternoon sun shone hotly on the deserted street, and low enough to create an uncomfortable glare from the west.

They stood waiting in the sun for twenty minutes, by which time Jones was becoming impatient.

'Where the hell is he?' he demanded, frustrated.

'He's not coming,' Casey mocked. 'Do you think he's stupid enough to walk into your silly little trap? You must be dumber than you look.'

Hot and angry, Jones stepped toward Casey and slapped her across her smiling face. With a yelp, she staggered slightly but remained upright. She lifted her head up and looked as though she might strike Jones back.

'Shut your mouth,' he hissed and moved out of reach.

'Gettin' a might jumpy, Delbert,' Lawson observed.

'Don't you start,' Jones snapped. 'He should have been here by now.'

'He's here,' Laredo theorized.

'Where?' Jones turned his head sharply.

'Who knows?' Laredo shrugged. 'But he's out there watchin' us.'

Jones snorted derisively. He looked about the deserted street and saw nary a sign of anyone.

'Is he right?' he shouted at nobody. 'Are you out there, Swift?'

'I'm here,' I called back.

All of them turned and looked into the blazing sun.

★   ★   ★

I left my horse on the outskirts of Big Springs, worked my way around to the west and climbed atop the flat roof of the dry-goods store. From behind its large false-front, with the sun at my back, I could see down along the main street using the glare to my advantage. I was careful to stay low so as not to throw a shadow, which might give my position away.

I watched them emerge from the jail and take up their positions. I could see Jones and Lawson along with two others standing with Casey. Laredo Mossop was under the awning out front of the jail while three other would-be bushwhackers found places to hide in various alleyways.

Then I waited. I wanted them to wait, to wonder what I was up to. The longer they waited the more agitated Jones became. Anger grew within me when I saw him strike Casey and I watched as she faced him defiantly after she'd gathered herself. When Jones called out to me I knew it was time.

'I'm here.'

They all turned to look. In doing so their eyes were assailed by the sun's fierce glare. Shading their eyes with their hands, they tried to see where I was.

'Where the hell are you? Are you on the dry-goods store?' Jones called out to me.

'Close enough to put a bullet between your damn eyes,' I shouted back. I lined the Winchester up on his head.

'Get your ass down here or I'll have one of my men here shoot the girl.'

Shifting my aim I lined the foresight up on the man standing on Casey's left. I squeezed the trigger and the Winchester bucked. The man dropped like a stone as the slug punched a hole in his head.

'*He* won't be doin' it,' I shouted when the echo had died away. 'Now let Casey go or I'll kill another one of you. I ain't made up my mind who yet.'

'Damn you, Swift!' Jones shouted, panic evident in his voice.

I fired again and the man to Casey's right dropped. I noticed that she flinched as the thunder of the gunshot rolled along the street. I saw Lawson move.

'Don't think about it, Lawson. I've got you covered.'

He froze but Laredo Mossop, thinking I couldn't see him, started to edge along the boardwalk. The Winchester spewed another lead missile and splinters flew from the awning post near his head.

'I'm gettin' hot up here, Jones,' I warned him. 'The next one has your name on it.'

There was a pause. Then I called out: 'Are you there, Chuck?'

Chuck stepped out on to the street holding a cocked six-gun. Jones stared at him, his face screwed up in anger.

'You work for me, damn it!' Jones cursed at him.

'I did, but once you'd paid me I started workin' for Swift.'

'Then you'll die too,' snarled Jones.

'Enough talk. Get her out of here, Chuck,' I ordered him.

He moved forward and grabbed Casey by the arm.

'C'mon, missy. Time we left.'

She took a lurching step and stopped. She looked in my direction.

'Go with him,' I called to her. 'He'll take care of you.'

Without a word she walked away with him. The last I saw, they were disappearing down an alley to where Chuck had horses waiting.

'That was smart,' Laredo Mossop called out from where he was standing. 'If I'd been you, I woulda picked my friends a little more cautiously.'

'What are you on about, Mossop?' I called back to him.

'That feller you just let go outta here

with the girl is Chuck Hollinger.'

I frowned. 'Yeah, so? Is that name meant to mean somethin' to me?'

'The man has a price on his head for robbin' stages and murder. His last job, he got most of his gang killed. Oh — I almost forgot — he also is wanted for forcin' himself upon a woman right before he cut her throat. Yep, mighty careless if you ask me.'

My mind reeled. If Laredo was to be believed, instead of saving Casey I'd put her in even more danger.

'What are you goin' to do now, Lightning?' Lawson shouted.

I raised my rifle and shot him in the face. Then Big Springs erupted in gunfire.

★ ★ ★

Casey stopped suddenly as the gunfire sounded from behind her. She turned to look back and took a hesitant step the way she and the man she knew as Chuck, had just come. A strong hand grasped her arm.

'Where do you think you're goin'?'

'We have to go back and help Billy,' Casey said, wrenching her arm free. 'We can't just abandon him.'

'He told me to get you outta town and that's exactly what I'm goin' to do,' Chuck told her.

'And go where?'

'His mine. He said it's in the Ajo Mountains.'

'But we have to help him,' she pleaded.

Once more, Chuck grabbed her by the arm. This time he wasn't letting go.

'You'll damn well do as I tell you. Now move,' he snarled.

Alarm registered on Casey's face and she remained fixed to the spot. Chuck poked the barrel of his six-gun under her chin.

'Move,' he snarled.

From the frying pan into the fire.

'Oh Lord, Billy,' she whispered. 'What have you done?'

Slugs chewed splinters from the top of the false-front where I was hiding, spraying them through the air, sharp and dangerous missiles. I rose up and fired another couple of shots from the Winchester at a man in an alley. He ducked back as my lead gouged chunks out of the plank wall where he sheltered.

Jones had taken cover behind a water trough; Laredo Mossop was behind a thin awning post. He didn't stay there for long because three well-placed rifle bullets made him duck back into the jail.

I shifted my aim back and fired relentlessly at the place where Jones was sheltering. Slivers of wood flew from the trough's side and small spouts of water shot upwards, indicative of my reasonable accuracy.

Lawson's body lay in the street near the two hired men I'd killed, his arms outstretched where he'd fallen. The remaining three hired men were still alive and firing wildly up at me.

A sliver of wood cut my cheek and a thin line of blood trickled to my jaw. I fired at the culprit and heard him yell as a bullet scored a deep furrow across his left arm. As I levered another round into the rifle's breech he lurched from cover enough for me to get a clear bead on him. The foresight came into line with his head and I squeezed the Winchester's trigger.

The hammer dropped but nothing happened. I cursed and ducked back as another fusillade of fire made a staccato noise on wood. Reaching into my pockets I found some more cartridges and fed them into the Winchester's magazine. It took what seemed to be an age to complete the task.

With a fresh round in the breech, I hooked around the end of the false-front to fire down upon Jones and his men once more. Except Jones was gone and the men in the alleyways had moved. It appeared that the time it took to reload when I ran out of ammunition was all they had needed to reposition themselves.

I glimpsed one as he disappeared down the alley beside the building on which I stood. Another had moved across the street, while Jones ran along the boardwalk seeking alternative cover.

Then I caught sight of Laredo Mossop. He'd managed to climb up on to the jailhouse roof. He opened fire and bullets snapped loudly as they fizzed past. More splinters flew from the false-front. I had to get off the roof before they had me pinned down.

As if on cue, a rifle opened fire from another roof across the way. The third man.

Well, now they had me pinned and it was about to get a lot worse. Something thudded on the roof and broke. I looked and saw that it was a clay jug. It was broken and liquid had spilled from it. I frowned but then the smell assailed my nostrils. Coal oil!

It didn't take long for a fiery torch to

follow it up. The oil caught instantly and flames licked greedily at the volatile liquid. The man I'd caught a glimpse of in the alley had no doubt set the fire that was now taking hold of the tinder-dry wood.

What to do? Now, as well as the heavy gunfire, I had this new danger to deal with. If I stayed where I was I would die. If I tried to get down I would most likely die. I didn't have time to die. I had to get Casey away from that damned killer I'd entrusted her to.

One thing was certain: I wasn't going to burn to death. I took one last look at the fire, which had now spread by more than double, black smoke billowing towards the sky. I tensed, then gripped the Winchester in my right hand and ran across the burning roof towards the side alley. I jumped.

16

When Delbert Jones saw Gray Lawson drop dead after the rifle shot smashed into his face, he dived behind the water trough and cowered there while bullets hammered the hell out of it. He drew his own small double-action Lightning .38 caliber revolver from its shoulder holster and started to return fire.

Its small sharp cracks sounded in sharp contrast against the sound of the heavier caliber guns. He stopped to reload, his mind running wild. Lawson and two of the men he'd hired were dead. Swift was pinned down on the roof and he was stuck behind the water trough. He saw Laredo driven back inside the jail, then the gunshots stopped.

'He's reloading,' one of the hired guns called out.

Not needing to be told twice, Jones

ran for the jail. Once inside he found Mossop standing at the front window.

'How the hell are we meant to get him off there without getting killed?' Jones asked, relieved that he was now safe from harm.

'Burn him off there?' Laredo suggested.

'And I know where to get the stuff to do it,' said one of Jones's hired guns, a man called Reece, from the doorway.

'Do it,' said Laredo. 'On your way there, tell Proctor to get up top. We'll keep his head down from there. Hurry.'

Reece disappeared and Laredo looked at Jones.

'Let's go.'

★　★　★

I crossed the gap between the two buildings easily. It was when I landed on the next roof that I had a problem. I went straight through it, feet first. It just gave way beneath me and before I knew it I was descending at a terrible rate.

When I landed, it was with a loud crash amongst a shower of dust and wood and bolts of cloth.

Groaning, I struggled to my feet and looked about. I figured I'd landed in a seamstress's shop.

Suddenly I stopped moving. Standing before me with a mortified look on her face was a middle-aged lady. Then I realized she wasn't alone: there were another two people with her. I reached up to touch the brim of my hat but found it wasn't there. I looked down at my feet, found it and rammed it back on my head.

'Are you OK, young man?' she asked in a not unconcerned voice.

'Sorry about the roof, ma'am,' I said. 'Back door?'

She pointed hesitantly towards the rear of the building.

'Thanks.'

My clothes were dusty and torn, I limped more than just a little and I had blood on me in quite a few places. But I still had my twin Peacemakers and the

Winchester was in my left hand. That meant I was still in the fight. All I needed now was to find my buckskin and get after Chuck and Casey.

No sooner had I burst out of the back door than I was confronted by one of Jones's hired men. He was standing, six-gun raised, looking up at the burning roof that I had recently vacated. Surprised, he spun toward me. His six-gun snapped into line with my chest.

It was more a reflex action than a conscious one when my right hand streaked down at the speed of a striking rattler. It came back up with a cocked Peacemaker and, as soon as I had it aimed, I squeezed the trigger. The slug hammered into his chest just as he fired his own gun.

His bullet flew wide, missing by at least two feet. There was no need to fire again for he was sinking to his knees, a large red stain already forming on his shirtfront.

Shouts sounded close so I holstered

the Colt and ran.

Hobbled was a more accurate description of what I was doing as I was still hurting from my ungraceful descent through the roof. I realized that I needed somewhere to hide — at least until after dark, anyway, so that I could slip out of town unseen and track down Chuck and Casey. She was my first priority; the others could wait.

When Irene Saunders answered her door, I could see the conflict in her eyes as an internal debate raged as to whether to let me in or not. When she saw that I was bleeding, however, there was no further hesitation.

'Quickly, come inside,' she urged me.

'I'm sorry to bother you, again,' I apologized. 'It'll only be until it gets full dark and then I'll be gone.'

'Let me take a look at those cuts,' Irene said. 'I'll clean them up for you.'

'They'll be fine, ma'am, I just need to hide out until dark.'

'Take a rest in the living room on the lounge. I'll be with you in a moment.'

I did as Irene said and found a seat on her lounge. Suddenly a whole wave of weariness washed over me. Even though I was on edge, by the time she came back I was asleep.

★   ★   ★

In my experience, there are two things that will snap a man from a deep slumber in the blink of an eye. One is a bunch of howling Apaches out to lift a man's hair. The other is a loud and sudden noise. The sound of the front door of Irene's small house crashing open and slamming against the hall wall did exactly that.

My hand immediately dropped to my right-side Colt. It came clear of leather and was on full cock before I had got to my feet.

'Where is he?' I heard Jones shout loudly as he barged into the hallway.

'He's not here,' came Irene's retort.

'He was seen, woman. There was a witness.'

I heard more voices and looked down at the six-gun I held in my hand. The sound of the extra voices made up my mind for me as I holstered the gun. I hurried toward the kitchen and out through the back door. The last thing I wanted was for a gunfight to break out in Irene's home and for her to catch a stray bullet.

The shadow of a man loomed in front of me.

'Hey!'

I brought up the Winchester and drove the stock into his midriff. With an audible whoosh, the air rushed from his lungs and he doubled over.

Breaking into a jog I headed for where I'd left the buckskin. Of course, it wasn't there. Why would it be? My conclusion was that they'd found it earlier and hidden it somewhere. So I'd have to steal one and worry about mine after I'd sorted this damned business out. At this time there was one place I could pick up a bronc; I headed that way.

When I made it on to the main street I found that there were three I could choose from. All were tied to a hitching rail outside the saloon.

I took the first one I came to: a sorrel. As I unhitched the reins a man came outside and looked me up and down.

'Hey, you can't take that horse,' he protested. 'It ain't yours. It's Philbert's.'

While I climbed into the saddle he poked his head back inside the saloon.

'Hey, Philbert,' he shouted above the noise, 'there's a feller out here tryin' to steal your horse.'

I was more than halfway along the main street of Big Springs when a flurry of gunfire broke out behind me.

★   ★   ★

Delbert Jones ripped the hat from his head and threw it into the dirt at his feet.

'I want that son of a bitch back!' he shouted in frustration. He whirled on the three men standing behind him.

213

'You useless — '

'Easy,' Laredo cautioned him, his voice chilly.

Jones's eyes fixed on him. His nostrils flared as he trembled with rage.

'You want him so bad,' he seethed, 'well here's your chance, big man. I'll pay you five thousand dollars to put him in the ground.'

Laredo nodded.

'I'd do it for free, but I'll take your money.'

'Good,' Jones snapped. 'And don't come back until the job is done. And take this useless pair with you. They might give Swift something to shoot at while you're sneaking up on him.'

Without another word he turned on his heel and stormed off. Laredo looked at the useless pair, Proctor and Tunks.

'You two stay the hell outta my way,' he warned them, 'or you'll end up like your friend Reece. Now get your damned horses.'

★ ★ ★

214

With the silvery glow of the full moon cast across the desert, Chuck Hollinger and Casey kept traveling in the direction of the Ajo Mountains. Big Springs was now six hours behind them and becoming more distant by the minute. For the past hour, Casey would have liked to wipe some of the trail dust from her eyes but, her hands being tied to the saddle horn, it was a bit difficult.

So on they rode, coyotes signaling their passage with lonesome howls and the great saguaros standing guard on their trail.

An hour or so after midnight Hollinger stopped to rest the horses. They found a place off the trail surrounded by palo verde bushes and some ocotillo. He dragged Casey from the saddle. She struggled and kicked at first but a brutal slap stopped her cold.

'Keep it up and the next one will be twice as hard,' he snarled.

Casey sat with her back against a rough-faced rock and watched as Hollinger made a small fire. He looked

215

up and saw her staring at him.

'What?'

'Why are you doing this?' she asked him. 'Billy would have paid you for what he asked.'

'He's been long dead by now, girl,' Hollinger told her. 'There was no way he was gettin' out of that town alive. So, I plan on takin' some of the gold for myself, then I'm headin' for good ol' Mex. And you're comin' with me.'

'What? You're crazy.' There was fear in her voice.

'Is that what you think? Girly, you are worth almost as much as gold below the border,' he told her. 'Yes, sir. You'll fetch a right nice price.'

The icy hand of fear gripped her heart at his words and she wondered if what he said was true. Would Billy come for her? Or was he already dead?

'You'd best get some sleep while you can, girly. We got us a long day tomorrow.'

17

The first pale orange rays of dawn were streaked with a purple hue that painted the desert in a myriad of spectacular colors. I figured there was still some distance to cover before I caught up with Chuck and Casey.

I climbed back aboard the sorrel after allowing him a rest just off the trail in the midst of a clump of rocks. Now that he was a little fresher for it, I hoped he would carry me on until I caught up with my quarry.

An hour later I found where they'd camped for some of the night. I sighted where they'd cut off the trail and set their fire, which was now scattered around where Chuck had kicked it out. Looking at the sign, I figured I was maybe two hours behind them.

Mid-morning brought me bad news. I topped a low ridge scattered with saguaro and palo verde and stopped to check my back trail. In the distance was a faint smudge of dust rising into the clear desert air.

Three, maybe four riders, I guessed.

I turned the sorrel and headed off along the trail. I needed to catch up to Chuck before whomever was behind me did the same to me.

The first faint hint of dust I caught was late in the afternoon. It was around a mile or so distant amid a rolling expanse of cactus and rock-strewn hills. I hoped to catch up just on nightfall; then, with dark for cover, I could surprise Chuck and get Casey back.

★　★　★

Casey was scared. Halfway through the afternoon Hollinger had produced a bottle of what he called 'snakehead' whiskey.

'D'you know why they call it that?' he'd asked her. 'It's because when it's made, they stick a couple of snake heads in the barrel to give it bite.'

Then he'd started drinking. With the drinking came the looks from him that made her feel nervous. Now, since making camp, he wouldn't stop staring at her.

From her side of the fire Casey watched him warily across the flames. The orange tongues reached up and little sparks floated off into the darkness. Every time he moved she became more on edge.

'You know, girly,' he slurred, raising the almost empty bottle. 'You're a mighty fine looker.'

Casey ignored him.

'Did you hear what I said?'

Again she ignored him.

Hollinger screwed up his face and spat in the sand where he sat, his back against a slab of rock.

'Don't you ignore me, girl,' he snarled. 'I won't be ignored. If I get up I'll come over there and teach you some manners. Damned if I won't.'

There was a pregnant pause before

he slurped down the last of the bottle.

'Hell!' he snorted. 'I might just do that anyway.'

Hollinger staggered to his feet and lurched around the fire towards her. His eyes were glassy and when the firelight caught them they gave off an eerie glint.

'You stay away from me,' Casey warned him. However, the fear in her voice was too pronounced for her words to worry the drunken outlaw.

She rose to her feet and started to back away, increasing the distance between them. Hollinger reached down and took a wicked-looking knife from his belt.

'Yeah, you and me is goin' to become real acquainted by the time the night is done.'

Hollinger held the knife at shoulder height and twisted it so that the light from the fire flickered from it. He kept walking toward Casey, who in turn continued to back away until she turned and ran.

'You can't go anywhere, girly,' Hollinger cackled maniacally. 'I'll find you and then I'll cut you good so you won't run away again.'

The desert was again lit by moonlight and, although not as brightly lit as the night before, it was certainly navigable. She knew that to run out into the desert without a horse or water was as good as a death sentence. So, instead of doing that, Casey circled the camp towards where the horses were tied, trying to keep out of sight by using the palo verde and rocks as much as she could.

'C'mon girly, come back,' Hollinger's voice was almost a whine. 'I ain't goin' to hurt you. I only want to be friendly.'

The horses appeared in front of Casey, hitched to a palo verde branch. She reached out to untie the reins to her mount when . . . 'Gotcha!'

A hand clamped on her wrist in a vicelike grip. She tried to wrench it free but it was no use. Hollinger dragged her close to him. His breath, reeking of alcohol, filled her nostrils.

'Let me go,' she squeaked, fear choking off her voice.

'Now, now,' he said, trying to calm her. 'It ain't goin' to hurt none. We'll just have us a little fun.'

As he leaned in close to try and kiss her Casey's fingernails raked his face, drawing blood in four open trails down his left cheek.

'Ow! You bitch!' Hollinger cursed as she broke free.

With all of her strength Casey swung at him with a closed fist. Her arm jarred all the way up to her shoulder as it connected with Hollinger's jaw with a meaty smack. He staggered back, trying to keep his balance.

Casey grabbed a handful of reins and ripped them free from the branch they were tied to. She had rushed forward to mount when Hollinger's hand took a grasp of her hair and hauled her backwards away from the horse. She screamed loudly, more from fear than pain.

Hollinger started to drag her back into the firelight. Casey fought and kicked to free herself but it was no use. Even in his inebriated state he was still stronger than she was. Once they were beside the fire he dropped her at his feet. He took off his jacket and threw it down beside him, then worked at his suspenders.

The first one was halfway down his left arm when the dry triple-click of a gun hammer going back made him freeze.

* * *

'If you keep goin' I'll shoot your pecker off and then gut shoot you and leave you for the buzzards.' My warning came out of the darkness beyond the firelight.

'Who . . . who's there?' Hollinger stammered.

'Is that better?' I stepped into the light.

'Billy!' Casey exclaimed.

'Stay where you are, Casey,' I ordered

223

her. My eyes never left Hollinger. 'You, on the other hand, take a few steps to your right.'

The Colt I had in my right hand tracked him as he moved.

'That'll do.'

'What now?' Hollinger asked.

'Now you go for that gun at your hip,' I told him, my voice cold.

'But you already got yours out and cocked,' he pointed out.

'Well,' I shrugged my shoulders, 'you better hope you're quick then, huh?'

'Hell! You gotta give me more of a chance than that,' Hollinger pleaded. 'For the love of God, it would be plain murder.'

'Go figure.'

He shook his head.

'One . . . '

'What are you doin'?'

'Countin'.'

'What for?'

'When I get to three I aim to kill you.'

'What?' Alarm spread across his face.

'You can't do that. You can't!'

'Two . . . '

'The hell with you!' His face screwed up into a vicious snarl.

He went for his gun, which I let him touch before I punched his ticket. The desert night was split apart when the Colt I held roared, spitting a tongue of orange flame from its barrel. The slug hit Hollinger in the chest, driving him back a couple of steps. He grunted audibly at its impact.

I shot him again at the thought of what he'd been about to do to Casey — and a third time just because I could. He fell with a dull thud on top of a prickly pear plant as dead as can be.

'Are you OK?' I shifted my gaze to Casey.

Before I knew it she was in my arms, almost knocking me off my feet. I had to catch myself before I fell over.

'Yes, yes!' she exclaimed. 'Now that you're here.'

Casey drew back and kissed me hard on the lips. I responded to her passion briefly, then pushed her away. She looked at me confused.

'What's wrong?'

'We gotta get out of here,' I answered. 'I got trouble on my back trail and the sound of those gunshots will act as an alert and guide them in here. Get your things together. I'll get my horse.'

I brought the sorrel into camp from where I'd left it and found Casey mounted and ready.

'How did you get away?'

'Long story . . . '

'We got time.'

I whirled around as out of the darkness came Laredo Mossop and the two hired guns. All held leveled weapons on us. My heart sank. After everything that had happened it all came down to this moment.

About to be shot down like a dog.

Laredo must have read my mind.

'Don't you worry none, Lightning,' he said. 'I ain't goin' to just shoot you. Nope. We're goin' to wait until sun up and then we're goin' to face off. Just you and me.'

'Why would you do that?'

'Admiration,' he said, surprising me. 'Every gun that has come after you, you've managed to put down. Hell, you even put down that bounty hunter, Murphy. He even gave *me* the creeps. Which proves how good you are. Nope, this is about reputation now.'

'Is that it? Is that all? What about your brothers?'

'What about 'em?' he asked with a shrug. 'Sure, it started out about them but what the heck! I'd have probably buried 'em myself by now. Oh — and there's the money side of it. Jones is now offerin' five thousand dollars for your scalp. He sure wants you dead.'

Laredo smiled in amusement. I, however, remained silent.

'Unbuckle them guns of yours and let 'em drop,' he ordered.

I didn't move.

'You'll get 'em back when the time's right,' he said. 'You don't think I'm goin' to leave them with you, do you? It's hours till dawn and you might get an idea about backshootin' me or some such.'

Again I hesitated.

'Proctor, shoot the girl.'

18

'Whoa! Hold on, Laredo,' I blurted out. I looked at Casey, who had a horrified expression on her face as she sat nervously on her horse. 'I'll do you a deal.'

'You ain't in no position to be makin' deals, Lightning.'

'Maybe not,' I allowed. 'Let Casey go.'

'Billy, no,' she protested.

'Now why would I do that?' He looked at me thoughtfully.

'You don't need her,' I pointed out. 'It's me you want. She ain't a threat to you.'

'What's she to you?.'

'Nobody,' I said coolly. I heard her gasp.

'You're lyin',' he said to me.

'She's nothin', Laredo.' I shook my head. 'You know men like us can't have somethin' like that tied around our necks. It causes weakness.'

'All right.' He nodded. 'Get her outta here.'

I walked over to the horse and looked up at Casey. Even in the poor light I could see the hurt in her eyes.

'I'm sorry, Casey,' I apologized.

She humphed at me and made to ride off. I snatched at the horse's bridle.

'Go to Irene's,' I said in a low voice. 'I'll find you there when this is over. Don't let Jones see you.'

In the fading campfire light I could see the sparkle of tears on her cheeks. She stared hard at me. 'You go to Hell, Lightning Swift,' she said through gritted teeth. With that, Casey kicked the horse hard and it lunged away into the night.

Turning back toward Laredo, I unbuckled my twin Peacemakers and let them drop.

He nodded.

'Good,' he said. 'Now get some rest. I

want you in top condition when the sun comes up.'

*　　*　　*

When the sun crowned over the horizon it bathed the desert first in red, and then orange. By the time Laredo was ready to have me face him over smoking guns, the air was clear and the heat was already scorching the sun-baked land.

Laredo approached me carrying my twin Peacemakers. He dropped them at my feet where I was sitting.

'It's time,' he said before walking back to the campfire to a brewing coffee pot.

I stood and buckled on my guns. I tied the rawhide thongs about my thighs and checked the loads in my six-guns.

'Do you want some coffee?' Proctor asked me.

'Sure, why not? After all, it may well be the last one I ever have,' I surmised.

'It will be,' Laredo chipped in.

'Tell me somethin', Laredo,' I said. 'Just supposin' I beat you. What happens then? With these two friends of yours, I mean.'

'They ain't my friends,' he said bluntly. 'And I guess that's up to them. I'm not them, mind, but you'll still be five thousand dollars on the hoof. Not that it matters any, 'cause you won't beat me.'

My gaze shifted across the rim of the coffee cup as I took a sip to study the faces of the other two men. They gave nothing away, but five thousand dollars was a lot of money so I guessed if I took down Laredo I would have to do the same to them.

'All right. How are we goin' to do this?' I asked Laredo. He pointed at his tin cup.

'I figured one of them could bang on this here cup as a signal. Can't be much fairer than that.'

'I ain't never figured that 'you' and 'fair' would associate much.'

Laredo tossed the dregs of his coffee on the fire making it sizzle.

'We don't.' He then threw the cup to Tunks. 'Let's get it done.'

I nodded and dropped my cup on the ground. We separated and when we were around fifteen feet apart we faced each other. I let my arms relax and my fingers dangle close to the twin Lightning Peacemakers. I took a deep breath, then let it out slowly. My eyes fixed on Laredo Mossop as I waited for the prearranged signal.

His face was all business. He'd done this many times; so, up until five years ago, had I. If ever my raw gun speed needed to shine through then it was now.

'Any time you're ready, Tunks,' he said grimly.

A surge of adrenaline swept through my body, making it tingle. No matter how fast you were, if you couldn't shoot straight you might as well throw rocks.

When the moment came it sounded as though a church bell had been rung, not a tin cup. My right hand dived for the Peacemaker. I don't think I've ever been faster. One fluid, smooth motion, and the Colt was out and roaring. I fired twice. Laredo lifted up on his toes as the slugs drove home. Two red stains appeared on the front of his shirt. He staggered about and his own six-gun fell from his hand. There was a thin wisp of gun smoke trailing from its barrel, indicating that he'd fired also.

Laredo Mossop, all six feet three of him, fell like a giant tree. He landed on his side with a dull thud.

I shifted my aim and brought the Peacemaker to bear on Tunks and Proctor. The thought of all that money was too much for Proctor. He had started his draw but he was a day too late.

The six-gun in my fist roared again and the slug hit where I aimed: his right shoulder was punched back by the impact. Nerveless fingers dropped his weapon into the dust at his feet.

My eyes locked on Tunks, who was

frozen to the spot. I could see that he wanted in but his indecision had cost him valuable time. With my Peacemaker on full cock I said:

'Make your choice. Buy in or take your friend there and ride.'

Even though he was staring down the barrel of a cocked six-gun he was still undecided.

'Is it worth your life?' I queried.

Eventually sense won out. He walked across to the wounded Proctor and helped him to his feet. I could see the sleeve of Proctor's shirt, soaked with blood.

'Be thankful it was your shoulder I aimed for and not your head,' I told him. 'Now the pair of you get on your horses and ride outta here. Not to Big Springs. If I ever see you there, I'll kill the pair of you.'

I watched them until they were gone, then I walked across to Laredo Mossop. I crouched over him and turned him from his side on to his back. Somehow the big killer was still alive. He moaned and his eyes flickered open. I could hear a gurgling sound in his chest when he breathed.

His eyes focused on me and he coughed, the rattle in his chest getting worse.

'I . . . I don't know how . . . how I missed,' he gasped.

Only then did I realize that I had a faint burning pain in my side. I looked down and saw the tear in my shirt was spattered with blood.

'You didn't miss,' I told him. 'You just didn't kill me is all.'

But he didn't hear me. Laredo Mossop, whom many had called the Gun King, was dead.

★   ★   ★

It was well after midnight when I reached Big Springs. The streets were deserted and the only living thing to greet me upon my arrival was a dog, which snarled, gave a couple of barks, then retreated into the shadows. I found Irene's house and went to the back

236

door. I could only hope that Casey had taken my advice to come here.

I banged on the door. It took a short while but eventually I heard her voice on the other side.

'Who is it?' she asked tentatively.

'Billy Swift,' I answered her.

The door opened and standing there was Irene in her dressing gown. Her face showed her concern and I knew instantly something was wrong.

'Thank God you're here!' she exclaimed. 'Jones has Casey. He caught sight of her coming into town and took her to the jail.'

I felt all sense of weariness from the trail leave me instantly. The news shook me and I realized just how deeply I cared for Casey.

'It doesn't stop, does it,' I mumbled.

'What?'

'The killing,' I elaborated. 'I'm tired of it. Once upon a time it didn't worry me. But since Mule died, and everythin' that's happened since then, I've had enough.'

'Then you go and save that girl and take her away from here,' Irene said sternly. 'Get far away. I know what that girl thinks of you and I'm sure you feel the same way.'

'I plan on doin' that,' I assured her. 'Just as soon as I deal with Jones once and for all.'

'You be careful,' she said.

'I'll be fine,' I told her and turned away.

★ ★ ★

I stood on the darkened street outside the jail and saw the faint light of the lamp inside that shone through a split in the window blind. I had no plan. I had no idea what to expect once I walked through the door but I'd soon find out.

My footfalls were light on the steps as I climbed them, trying not to give away my presence too soon. I crossed the boardwalk and stopped outside the door. My left hand I placed on the door handle while my right gripped the butt of my Peacemaker. I turned the handle slowly until it would go no further. Then I took a deep breath, pushed the door open, and walked inside.

Delbert Jones was sitting in the chair behind the sheriff's desk, on top of which was a full glass of whiskey, a half-empty bottle, a messenger gun, and the lamp that was giving off a dim light. He didn't move, but watched as I crossed the room.

'I was expectin' you,' he stated. 'Somethin' just didn't feel right. Somehow I knew.'

'Billy!' Casey called from the cell where she was locked in.

Without taking my eyes from Jones I called out to her.

'Are you OK?'

'I'm fine. I'm mighty glad to see you, though.'

'I'll have you out in a minute.'

Jones showed a wan smile and I could tell I was looking at a defeated man. He leaned forward with his hand out, reaching. My right-side Colt leaped into my hand and I eared back the hammer.

He froze briefly and looked in my direction. Then he kept moving and took up the glass of whiskey. After a sip, he looked at me again.

'Mossop and the others?' he asked.

'Laredo's dead,' I told him. 'The others are a long way from here.'

He nodded.

'Was it worth it?' I asked.

'Was what worth it?'

'Your greed.'

'It would have been,' he said, leaning forward to place the now half-empty glass back on the desk. 'If you had just died!'

His last words were more of a snarl. As he said them he snatched at the messenger gun. It was the futile gesture of a man who figured he was going to die anyway.

I squeezed the trigger as his hand clamped on the gun to pick it up. The Colt thundered and the .45 caliber slug slammed into his chest. He half-rose out of the chair, then toppled sideways. He hit the floor and didn't move.

I closed the gap between us and stood over him. His eyes were wide open in death, the spark of life gone from them, snuffed out in one fleeting moment. At last it was over.

Casey!

I took the keys down from their peg and unlocked the cell Casey was in. She flew through the door and almost knocked me over, locking her arms around my neck. She kissed me long and hard. When we finally came up for breath Casey stepped back and looked into my eyes.

'Tell me it's over.'

'It's over,' I assured her. 'This part, anyway.'

'What do you mean?' She looked confused.

'When word spreads that I'm alive and I killed Laredo Mossop, every two-bit gun in the territory is goin' to come lookin' for me.' I sighed. 'I have to leave.'

'But why?'

'It's the only way.'

'Where will we go?'

'We?'

'You don't think I'm going to lose you now, do you? Mister, you're stuck with me,' she stated.

'I like the sound of that.' I smiled broadly. 'How do you feel about Montana?'

Casey smiled back at me.

'I like the sound of that.'

*   *   *

Two days later we left Big Springs. We rode out to the mine that Mule and I had shared and I worked for a few days, digging enough gold to tide us over. From there we rode north until we found a broad valley with a small town. There we began a life together as husband and wife on a small horse ranch, with a mule named Rosie.

But that is another story.